ALISTAR
A Colorful Journey

REEMA K. C.

BALBOA.PRESS
A DIVISION OF HAY HOUSE

Balboa Press books may be ordered through booksellers or by contacting:

Balboa Press
A Division of Hay House
1663 Liberty Drive
Bloomington, IN 47403
www.balboapress.com
1 (877) 407-4847

Interior Image Credit: Chris Hunter

Print information available on the last page.

ISBN: 978-1-9822-4353-1 (sc)
ISBN: 978-1-9822-4355-5 (hc)
ISBN: 978-1-9822-4354-8 (e)

Library of Congress Control Number: 2020903514

Balboa Press rev. date: 03/23/2020

To the young boys and girls who dare to
dream outside of society's norms.

Alistar is a likable boy with profound feelings and a penchant for art. Reema does well to inspire young readers to experience life from the point of view of Alistar, allowing the reader to relax and savor their own artistic beckoning.

-Paul Paiva
Father & Life Coach

The description of this charming, colorful environment instantly captures the reader's imagination. We are transported to Creatopia and into the harmonious existence created by King Zazar, which abruptly ends with his death, causing the seeds of selfishness and greed to foster in this once beautiful and enchanted Creatopia. The author draws us into this world of fantasy while the characters are very human like by their thoughts and actions. There is something in it for everyone.

-Kartika Muthu
Mother & Educator

Contents

Acknowledgments

Life is not always black and white. I want to acknowledge my family and friends who have encouraged me and helped me through this journey of releasing my first book. It has truly been a labor of love, and if just one boy or girl feels inspired by it, then it will have met its purpose.

CHAPTER 1

A Flame that Never Dies

"He's gone," Hemsworth whispered to himself as he gazed at the flames in his fireplace. It was a cold fall night in Hummingbird Forest. The rain dropped like rocks against his rickety tin roof. Hemsworth was preparing for the first day of a quest that he hoped would go down in the history books of the great Creatopia nation. His heart, like that of King Zazar's, desired harmony for the creatures that inhabited the land. *It wasn't always like this. Why did things have to get so bad?* He pondered the question as he reached into his cabinet above the stove and began to prepare a cup of maple leaf tea. The smell of the maple leaves brought back memories of sitting at King Zazar's round table, discussing the next big quest for Creatopia. Meetings always started off with a fresh pot of tea, served with crumpets made by the best chefs in Lemur Landing.

It had been a few years since the passing of King Zazar. Hemsworth turned to a photo on his fridge, which showed him sitting proudly on the shoulder of his beloved king. Zazar was known to have a radiant personality, always looking for ways to bring creatures of Creatopia together in harmony. The king had a crafty ability to look into the soul of any being. It was the words he chose to speak that pulled at a creature's heart strings. Zazar was a lemur of passion, honor, and justice. As one of the few lemurs left in Creatopia, he loved to dress in colorful velvet cloaks made of beads and jewels. At first, it was his sense of style that caught the eyes of many, but it was his personality that convinced them to stay. The photo was taken at Narwhal Landing when King Zazar spoke to the Narwhalians of joining the United Creatopia Kingdom. It was a day of victory, a day of pride, he thought silently to himself. Hemsworth was shocked to hear the news of King Zazar's passing. The two of them weren't just friends, they were like brothers. King Zazar's rule over the kingdom meant a future filled with great possibilities for Hemsworth and for Creatopia That is the thing about loss; it takes one down a deep hole into the darkness. One doesn't feel just a loss but also a sense of having to pick up the pieces of the past and somehow form them into a new future.

Hemsworth sat in his room for days, in the darkness, thinking only of how *he* could put the pieces together again. As the days passed, Hemsworth began to regain his strength and accept the emptiness that filled his heart. He then chose to honor his king by keeping memories of Zazar around the house and cherishing all the happy times they shared.

Although King Zazar always preferred to wear the finest velvet cloaks adorned with jewels and beads, he requested to be dressed in plain white cotton on the day of his departure. Each kingdom was asked to bring soil, feathers, and flowers from their homeland. With a fire burning and stories shared, all the kingdoms stood united behind the greatness of their beloved King Zazar.

Knock, knock, knock.

The sound of someone knocking at the door drew Hemsworth out of his daydream. He opened the door and peered out into the forest.

"Hello … you there?" Hemsworth called out into the night air. The rain fell heavily on the redbrick doorstep as he surveyed the dark forest.

Standing silently in the night rain, Hemsworth made out the figure of a mysterious visitor dressed in an emerald-green cloak.

"You have the vials?" the creature demanded in a low, raspy voice.

"Yes … yes … here they are." Hemsworth reached into his robe pocket and handed him four vials filled with bubbling liquids of various colors. The hooded creature grabbed the vials with his wet claws and turned quickly, returning to the woods.

"The night is growing tired. Be safe out there, my friend!" shouted Hemsworth as he watched the creature disappear into the darkness, riding swiftly on his raganoo. Hemsworth sat back down on his chair with a sense of hope and relief as he watched the last ember in the fireplace slowly burn itself out.

CHAPTER 2

Take Rest, My Sweet King

Take rest, my sweet king.
You shall not be forgotten,
For you have lived a life of glory,
With heart, with joy, with passion.
You are the soil, the grass, the roots
From which new fruits flourish.
Take rest, my sweet king.
You shall not be forgotten.

D eep in the redwoods of Hummingbird Forest, high above the tallest tree, sat a stately owl observing all that was above and all that was beneath the realm. He spread his wings and drifted down from his perch to land at a mystical pond that glistened in the night shadows. Moonbeams bounced off the surface of its waters and performed a dance for all creatures to enjoy. The hummingbirds filled the air with song created by the flapping of their tiny wings. It was one of the many sights to be seen in the magical kingdoms of Creatopia.

Palace Pond was brought to life in the pioneer days when Creatopia first began to form. One day, after a day of traveling, King Zazar decided to rest under a willow tree. As he sat on the soft grass and leaned back against the brittle bark of the tree, a vision emerged as he drifted off to sleep.

Zazar saw himself not just governing his small domain but leading all kingdoms in every corner of the land. It was his destiny to forge a pact of unity with all creatures under a United Kingdom of Creatopia. Before him, a grand plan appeared that would bring together all that lived in the lush green lands, the cool waters, and the deep blue sky. In his vision, he saw a pond filled with crisp, clean water, surrounded by giant lily pads. He could see that the life force of this great kingdom would be led by colorful beauty. His dream was quickly swept away when he was awoken by the nudging of his raganoo.

Everyone in Creatopia knew a raganoo was a cross between a peacock and a horse. Like the peacock, it had a sharp beak and could fan its tail in a display of color. Like the horse, it had a broad back, thick neck, and four strong legs like a stallion. A raganoo was clearly one of the fastest creatures on land and in the air. Like both the horse and peacock, they were intelligent creatures that became close confidants to their owner when nurtured and trusted. For these reasons, raganoos were one of many protected creatures in Creatopia.

After waking the king from his dream, the raganoo drifted away toward a long, leafy shrub. The king was curious after his raganoo awoke him and followed him into the forest. Soon, King Zazar found himself standing at the very same bank of the deep blue pond he saw in his dream. The pond was surrounded by the same pink lilies and the same glistening blue shrubs. Amazed by the sight, Zazar whirled around in circles as he soaked in the reality of his vision. Now he knew his destiny and the destiny of all creatures in Creatopia. Quickly, the king jumped onto his raganoo and flew like the wind to announce his grand plan to bring his vision to life.

As many moons passed, the king welcomed creatures from all

the lands to Creatopia. Five prominent kingdoms formed under King Zazar's rule: Palace Pond, Narwhal Landing, Carrot Kingdom, and Kiwi Country, not to mention Lemur Landing, the kingdom that led the others. What was once a land of separation, starvation, and greed became a land of opportunity through connection and empathy. The creatures began to connect and learn from one another, and the idea that all were different and needed to fend for themselves began to fade away. With this new nation forming, the creatures began to inspire one another and step into creativity and out of fear. The king was no longer dreaming under the willow tree; Creatopia was reborn with a new vision. Zazar wanted all creatures to live in a land not only of beauty but of heart and strength—a land built for all to share in harmony, free of judgment and division. He believed that acceptance and cooperation would lead to further greatness.

It was during his last few years of life that King Zazar made provisions to keep his legacy alive after his departure. He secretly appointed a caretaker to follow through with his wishes for the kingdoms. The king and caretaker planned for Creatopia to grow in grandeur long after his passing.

When King Zazar passed away in his sleep, the news quickly swept out to the surrounding kingdoms. In time, the rise of scarcity divided the kingdoms, and gaining wealth soon became the way to happiness. The life forces of beauty and heart that once blew through the winds over Creatopia were suddenly silenced by greed.

Lemur Landing was the first to fall under the strain of selfishness. Most all the inhabitants left homes to escape the unrest and division. There were a few brave creatures that stayed to protect the kingdom. It was in the time that the Ministry of Creatopia was created.

CHAPTER 3

Tools for My Toolkit

The sound of drums beating in the distance grew louder and louder. I spun around, wondering if there was any light anywhere. How could there be such absolute darkness? Where had the stars and the moon gone? Were we being punished for something? The night enveloped the forest with its brooding sense of the unknown. With bated breath, I looked around for a sign. Help.

Beep. Beep. Beep.

I could hear my alarm going off as I felt around my nightstand table, trying to turn the darn thing off. A gift from Mrs. Gringalgool, my sixth-grade history teacher.

"Alistarrrrrrrrrr! Wake up!" yelled my father. It was the first day of school.

Thank God that was just a dream, I thought. I could still feel the dream lingering in my mind as I tried to get back to reality. *It's time to take three deep breaths*, I thought. It was something my father taught me for when I woke up in a panic, looking around for him.

"There, there, Alistar. Remember what I told you: three deep breaths, and all is back to normal." My father, Jed Sparks, one of the most celebrated photographers and spiritual advisors that ever graced the earth, gave me that golden piece of advice. He was always trying to get me to do things that "helped my spirit." He firmly believed that we are here as spirits, and Mother Earth or nature has given us our rabbit bodies as vessels.

Most of my summer was spent redecorating my room, like I did *every* summer. This year I wanted to emphasize cool tones. I had a whole under-the-sea thing going on with narwhals plastered all over the walls of my room. There wasn't a store that sold what I was looking for, so I had to make the narwhals, but I didn't mind one bit. Going through the biggest arts and craft store and making my way through the glossy, white-tiled floor while looking at all the colors pop from shelves was like heaven on demand. There was a section of just glitter and beads. I did go a little crazy stocking up on the glitter, but, hey, it was a boy's dream to have everything and anything sparkly. One day I'm sure I'll use all this color. As I opened all the colored pencil boxes, I felt like I was the sharp-pencil inspector. The construction paper section was probably my favorite. It was always amazing to see the strength of the construction paper. It had a durable quality to it that I truly admired.

Everyone knew me at Mr. Toddly's House of Arts and Crafts, the local buy-all art and craft store in my neighborhood. The owner was Mr. Smorton, who used to be a good friend of my mother's. He was a chubby fellow and had a cup of tea swinging around in his hand all day as he talked. I would say he spoke a bit too close for comfort for the local customers who walked in the door. Needless to say, the store was the light of his life.

I always felt bad for Mr. Smorton. I could tell business was going downhill for him ever since King Tia increased the taxes in his store. It wasn't about the money; the store just made him happy when customers were around looking to make great creations using only their imaginations. The day after the last day of school, I lugged around almost everything in sight at Mr. Smorton's shop. There I was, getting ready to pay when I heard, "No, no, Alistar. Your mother would kill me if she knew I charged you anything. This one is on the house." Mr. Smorton was always telling me stories of my mother and how she was one of the best teachers the store had for their knitting classes.

"Go on now. Not to worry! This one is on the house," he repeated. I thanked him profusely, loaded what felt like thirty pounds of supplies onto my bike, and happily rode home.

"Alistar, come on. You'll be late for your first day of class!" my father urged, walking into my room, looking down at his watch. This had become our routine, and I think he enjoyed on some level that I was always late. It always gave him a reason to come by my room to check on me. It was a time we could connect for even just a moment before he had to head out to Carrot Kingdom to start his day of photographing. King Tia had hired my father as his personal photographer. He was to take pictures of King Tia throughout the day, doing "nice things" for the community. We all knew it was a crock of carrots, but it paid the bills, and that's all that mattered.

"I have something for you. Come down, and I'll show you." I knew what it was, but as was tradition, I wanted to keep him thinking that I didn't know. I could smell the sweet scent of birthday pancakes trailing up the stairs all the way to my room. It was one of our oldest family traditions.

"All right, Dad. Just one moment, and I'll be right down," I said while trying to put on my blue jeans that were draped over my desk chair from the night before. Luckily, I still fit into them. I hadn't had much of a growth spurt and was hoping it would kick in sometime this year. I opened my closet doors to find my babies all lined up—neat, crisp, and clean. They were my pride and joy. I had been going to the local thrift shops and collecting unique T-shirts in nearly every color. Every time I found a piece, I would inspect it to see if it had a certain quality. It had to be *unique*, or it just couldn't come home with me.

I picked out a white T-shirt that I had found just last week. It had a pocket at the top, right side with a blue dragonfly embroidered on it. This was such a subtle unique piece that I just had to have it. I threw on my T-shirt, followed by my favorite black leather jacket, and headed down the stairs.

We lived in a modest redbrick, two-story home with red shag carpets and dark cherrywood paneling along the walls. My baby pictures were, of course, plastered all over the living room walls. My dad photographed me standing next to our sunflowers in the front yard, which are still as tall as I am. The photographs were set in a black-and-white style finish, with a splash of yellow color just hitting the sunflowers. My dad and I are both artistic, although I feel like he downplays it a bit from time to time. The rest of the house hadn't been redecorated in a while. It was like Dad wanted to keep everything just the way it was. To change it would be *too much*. My mother had picked out the carpeting and paneling for the walls, so that wasn't going anywhere anytime soon.

"Mmmm … Dad, this is really good," I said while stuffing my mouth with my birthday pancakes and confetti frosting.

"You like it? I didn't do much, but I'm glad you like it." He was always fishing for compliments when it came to his cooking. I guess he didn't ever feel like he was doing a good job.

"Dad, seriously, these pancakes are everything!" I said, reaffirming to him that they were, in fact, the most delicious pancakes I'd ever had in my life. I always had to reinforce how much I loved things with my dad. He was just trying to make sure I was okay and still felt new at this dad thing, I guess.

"Give me!"

"What are you talking about?" my dad asked, smirking.

"Come on, Dad. I don't want to be late for my first day of school. Just give me what's mine," I growled, growing impatient. I had waited three hundred and sixty-five days for this and wasn't in the mood for my dad's shenanigans.

"It's right next to you," my dad said, laughing at my inability to see the wrapped, bright, lime-green gift in the empty chair next to me.

I pushed my plate with the leftover funfetti frosting aside and placed my lime-green gift box on top of the table. I could tell my dad did the wrapping because he didn't quite finish the job. There was this thing he did where he would cut the wrapping paper a little too short, and it wouldn't cover the whole gift.

"Alistar, take your time opening it," my dad prompted as I ripped through his poorly wrapped gift.

It was a clear acrylic box with a silver handle on it. There was a knitting set in there with lots of yarn in all the colors. I was mesmerized by the bright yellow yarn and how the color nearly leapt out of the acrylic box.

"It belonged to your mother," my dad said, picking up the dishes and getting ready to wash them in the sink. "There is a note there too. You can read it when you're ready. It doesn't have to be now."

My dad always got busy with housework right after the gift opening. He didn't want to be a part of giving me the gift. My mother was known as the knitter around town. She could knit nearly everything and anything. She too was an artist, like Dad and I.

"Thank you, Dad, for everything. I love the gift," I said, trying to reaffirm to him that everything was going well. I quickly picked up the card and put it in my backpack.

I was about nine months old when she passed away. My father never could tell me what happened, but Maribella did. One day she overheard her mom talking on the phone to one of her friends about it. My mom had fallen ill and suddenly passed. She must have known she was going because she did write me a birthday card for every year, supposedly, until I turned eighteen.

"Okay, I'm heading out now. Do you need a ride to school?" My dad always asked me if I wanted a ride to school, and I always declined. I preferred walking and taking in the beautiful scenery of Redwood Road. There was something therapeutic about seeing the tall redwoods along the road and breathing in the fresh morning air.

"No, Dad. I'm gonna walk today. I want to meet up with Maribella."

"Oh, I'm sorry I didn't tell you. Her mother called me last night and said she isn't going to be at school today. Said she wasn't feeling well."

Surprise, surprise, I thought. Maribella had done this same routine every year since the second grade. She always had an excuse to miss the first day of school. I think it's because she was anxious about what the new school year would bring.

"Okay. Thanks, Dad. No worries," I said, heading out the door.

"Have a good day. And, Alistar! Don't forget to stay on the path," my dad said sternly as I shut the kitchen door behind me.

CHAPTER 4

The Disappearing Act

As I stepped out of the house, I could feel the cool morning air against my tiny, pink, wet nose. My nose wasn't like the other rabbit boys. The pink color made me stand out against the others. It made me feel like I wasn't masculine enough. The other rabbit boys had darker noses than I did. Johnny's nose was black. Obviously, he thought it was much better than mine. It was so funny how the color of my nose made me feel. It wasn't something I could change.

Dad said to stay on the path, so stay on the path I would. He was talking about Redwood Road that was parallel to Hummingbird Forest. It was best to keep out of Hummingbird Forest, he would say. I was always tempted to go and explore. There was something majestic about watching hummingbirds flapping their wings high above the trees. As majestic as some of the creatures may have been, it didn't make being in the forest any safer. Through the years, some royals who belonged to Carrot Kingdom had disappeared. Every time King Tia would appoint a new guard to be by his side, they would mysteriously disappear. I think they must have just run away to one of the other many kingdoms. King

Tia was a difficult man to work with, from what I could tell. He was always having his guards go bee hunting for him, whatever that meant. He had this honey farm that he was so proud of.

He worked the bees day and night. Many of them would die, and he would have his guards clean out the cage. The faithful bees would go right into the trash, and then his guards would scavenge for more.

Not good juju, I thought. It was never a good thing to take so much from somebody that they had nothing left to give, and King Tia was notorious for that. I wish my father would stop working for him.

I was just passing Maribella's home when I noticed her mom getting in the car to head to work. *Should I go and say hello to her?* I thought. *No. If I do that, then she'll make it a whole big thing and probably freak me out for the first day of school.* I loved Maribella, but sometimes I wished she would just get a grip on reality. She lived in a place I called the "anxiety trap." It referred to when your mind starts going in a certain direction, it can spiral out of control, and as a seventh grader, you should really get a grip on things, or the world will eat you alive.

Maribella's mom was on the richer side of town. She drove an expensive car and always had these colorful power suits on with her pumps. Today, she was wearing a hot pink one. She surely stuck out like a wildflower in this overcast weather. *Oh, God. She's spotted me.*

"Alistar! Hello! How are you? You've grown so much" Gosh, I loved Maribella's mom, but boy, was she a talker. I learned to quickly cut things off with her.

"Hi, Mrs. Stagger! It's so nice to see you. Is Maribella doing okay? Dad told me she wasn't feeling well."

I knew what it was, but I had to ask just to ask.

"Yeah ... poor thing was up all night sick. I think she must have eaten something. Over dinner, we were talking about expectations and all the new things that were going to be happening, and suddenly she felt sick and went to her room."

Couldn't Mrs. Stagger see that she prompted Maribella's sickness?

She should have known that talking about all the new things would bring her into her anxiety trap, but I didn't say much because, like my father, Mrs. Stagger was a single parent. Widowed to be exact. Maribella's father passed away in the line of duty when she was three years old.

I felt bad because he didn't get to leave her anything since it was sudden. Mrs. Stagger blames King Tia to this day. She blames all of the kingdoms for not keeping their promise.

"All right, Alistar. I have to head to work, but I'd like for your father and you to come to dinner."

"Sure thing," I said, waving to her as she headed out the driveway and down to Carrot Kingdom. I wasn't going to deliver the message to my father, because I already knew the answer. He would say yes, and then he would come up with some excuse not to go. He always did that. It was like he felt guilty for going to dinner or even having a good time without Mom. All I could do was support him. *In his time, he will heal,* I thought.

Hummingbird Forest stretched for miles and miles, all the way to Vennister Middle School. It was always tempting not to hop the wooden fence and head in for a quick look around.

I knew that there were burnaberry trees close enough to Redwood Road for me not to get caught up in anything. Burnaberries are the absolute best. They are these very large berries the size of an apple. They are similar to raspberries and blackberries and taste just like cotton candy. It was a hint of sweetness just before the sour punch kicked in. Dad would always bring me some from work as a treat. King Tia had them planted right outside his castle. It was a bit chilly out, and I placed my paws in my jean pockets. I felt around the inside of my pockets, in admiration of the seamstress who probably sewed the inner lining together so finely. It took time, dedication, and talent. Something felt off as I dug around deep in my pockets. Oh no! I left the house so quickly I didn't think to ask my dad for lunch money. Perhaps there would be some change in my backpack.

I knelt down to open my backpack and see if he had left anything in there. Reaching around the very bottom of my bag, I managed to pull out a penny, lint, and a paperclip. *I'll need that for later*, I thought. I already knew that, when lunchtime rolled around, I could not watch the other kids eat while I sat hungry, waiting for the next period bell to ring, and Maribella wasn't there. No, hunger was not going to be an option.

I hopped over the wooden fence, disobeying my father's strict orders to stay on the path. *Hey, he forgot my lunch money*, I thought, *and a boy has got to eat.*

I walked through the forest, still staying within view of the road. There was now a plethora of cars beginning to slow down. That meant traffic was beginning to back up since it was the first day of school. I went deeper into the forest. I didn't want anyone to see me, or they might try to talk me out of going any farther into the forest, and I needed to find burnaberries to put in my backpack for lunch.

The overcast sky cleared, and the sun's warmth embraced me. I never felt alone walking in the sunlight. The road disappeared behind me as I walked toward what appeared to be a willow tree. The tree looked like it had dried up, incomparable to the lush green life that surrounded it.

This seems odd, I thought, and I kept walking as I spotted what looked to be the burnaberry tree Johnny Jester had bragged about. One day, he had come into class with a backpack full of fresh burnaberries. He said that he had gone into the forest and grabbed them. He was the only one brave enough to do anything like that.

I started stuffing my backpack with the burnaberries from the tree when something in the bushes moved.

I didn't think much of it and started filling my bag with the last few pieces that were around. The wind had started to pick up, and I heard the leaves begin to rustle through the trees.

"Alistar …" a raspy voice whispered from behind one of the trees.

Feeling panic set in all over my body, I felt paralyzed. *Are the trees talking to me or am I imagining things?*

"Alistar …" again a raspy voice whispered from one of the trees. *Is someone here?* The bushes began to shake as fear began to settle into my body. *I knew I shouldn't have come to this place.* If I listened to my dad, I could probably make it back home. *Always stay on the path*, I thought. *Stay on the path.*

A raganoo jumped out from behind one of the tall bushes and was now towering over me. Oddly, my fear began to slip away as I looked into the raganoo's soulful eyes, which gazed back at me.

I had never seen one up close before. There weren't many around anymore. Its coat was dark brown and short haired and shined in the sunlight. Its eyes were chestnut brown and sparkled in the sunlight.

I picked the berries out of my backpack and held out my palm. It took the fruit from my hand and, with one big chomp, broke it into tiny pieces and splattered the juices and pieces on the ground.

Dad wouldn't let me have a pet, and I felt like this was the closest thing to it.

"I'm gonna call you Chompers," I said to the raganoo, who seemed to be busy rummaging through my backpack. He was certainly a beauty.

Oh, crap! I'm late! Again!

I grabbed my backpack, waved goodbye to Chompers, and ran back toward the main road. I looked back to wave once more to my new friend, but just like that, Chompers had disappeared.

CHAPTER 5
Something's Brewing

I t was way too early for my floppy ears to hear the kettle whistling. How on earth did Mrs. Gringalgool manage to swing a tea-making class as part of the curriculum? I mean, come *on*. There isn't much to making tea. It's just water and leaves and stuff, but no. She had us studying the art of making tea. I mean, were we going to get tested on it?

Mrs. Gringalgool had no sense of style. I could see from the third row of our small trailer classroom that she hadn't put much effort into her outfit. She was wearing a pastel-green cardigan with brown shorts and a red top underneath. Everything screamed no-go to me, but I knew she had tried. She even managed to put on some earrings that I thought did give the outfit a certain pop, but, come on, Mrs. Gringalgool. Learn to color coordinate.

I could even see that there was a small tear in her cardigan. Everything about that outfit screamed help to me. I had an emergency sewing kit in my backpack that I kept just in case, for these types of outfit emergencies.

"Okay, everyone. Now it's time to take the teapot out. You'll know when it's time because the water will be boiling. You'll want to steep the tea for two to three minutes. This is the lemon herbal tea. It is to rejuvenate you and is made with properties that are healing for the mind, body, and soul."

Sometimes I thought Mrs. Gringalgool and my dad would get along. They were both into the healing powers of tea and nourishing the spirit.

Most of the boys in the class were groaning that they had to learn how to make tea.

"Mmmmm, you smell that? It's so earthy and should help most of you wake up for the next thirty minutes."

Mrs. Gringalgool had put this class into motion because she could see that our community was becoming all about money. King Tia had implemented higher taxes and was working on bringing in more jobs for the community, but what that really meant was longer hours. It was like everyone in this kingdom was turning into zombies, and Mrs. Gringalgool was just trying to combat that by bringing us back to being grounded. The idea was that learning to take a moment and have tea would calm the body before the business of school began and we got carried away in our work.

Ironically though, this class had assignments—and *a lot* of them.

When the bell for the next period rang, I couldn't help myself. I walked toward Mrs. Gringalgool with one thing in mind.

"Ahh, hello, Alistar! So good to see you!"

"Hi, Mrs. Gringalgool. Sorry for being late again. I ... ah ... had a wardrobe malfunction this morning," I said, lying through my tiny teeth. "I noticed during class that you had a small tear on your cardigan. Do you mind if I help you?"

Mrs. Gringalgool took a moment to realize what I was asking and robotically handed me her sweater to fix. I examined the tear closely; it was about half an inch and circular in size. I couldn't imagine how the tear even occurred.

"It's not going to look brand-new, but I'll do the best I can. Just a few moments."

Mrs. Gringalgool just smiled as I worked away.

I pressed together the two ends of where the fabric ripped and began to sew. I had almost every color of thread in my kit, and one matched Mrs. Gringalgool's outfit perfectly. I took thin thread and pushed it through the hole of the needle. With a steady hand and concentration, I began to swiftly push and pull the needle from the ends of the torn fabric, sewing it back together again seamlessly. My skill was different from those of the boys who walked the halls of Vennister Middle School. I preferred rainy days, playing with color for sport rather than throwing a ball around.

"There!" I said proudly as I handed Mrs. Gringalgool her cardigan.

There was something almost magical to me about taking something broken and fixing it up. Mrs. Gringalgool looked at her sweater and sighed in relief.

"Oh, thank you so much, Alistar. I have a few parent-teacher conferences, and I don't want anyone complaining about me looking stressed and disheveled."

Oh, I knew how some of the parents could be. Especially Johnny Jester's parents. It's like they had no compassion and no control, and Johnny was almost no different.

"Let me see," said a voice from behind. It was Johnny. He hadn't left the class. I guess he wanted to stay behind for more material to make fun of me for later.

"Oh wow. That looks really great, Alistar," he said sarcastically. I knew he was just trying to get under my skin. The nicer he pretended to be, the more the teachers didn't notice. It was like he had cast a mystical spell over them, hiding his true nature.

"Here you go, Mrs. Gringalgool. You keep this." I handed her my sewing kit and headed out the door. I was not in the mood to entertain

Johnny's sarcasm. He would find me later for sure. Today, I was just not in the mood.

"Hey, you dropped this." Mrs. Gringalgool ran up behind me, trying to catch up, holding a piece of crumpled paper. I didn't recognize that it belonged to me, as I kept all of my assignments neatly tucked away in my binder.

"I don't think that's mine," I said to her.

She held out the crumpled paper on her paw. "I hope you don't mind. I just glanced at it for a second. Are you taking poetry? It's pretty good."

She straightened out the piece of paper a little more and handed it to me.

Before the Sunflowers Rise

She sings to the flowers,
Her coat as bright as the sun.
She jumps in the sunlight
Before the troubled night begun.
There is sweetness in the songs.
There is sweetness all around.
The sweetness seeps deep,
Deep into the ground.
He took from her
With greed in sight.
She sits in sadness,
Now brewing anger inside.
One day she hopes again she will rise.
Until then, she only feels despise.

Ringggggggg! The bell rang for the next period.
"Oh, crap! I'm late again!"

CHAPTER 6

The Powerful Gift

"Maribella!"

I couldn't scream any louder. We were about to be late, and Mrs. Stagger had already left for work. Maribella had barricaded herself in the house. She did not want to go to school, and I wasn't about to go through another school day without her.

"Maribella! Maribella! Maribella!"

Passersby in their cars stared at me as I stood on Maribella's lawn, screaming at the top of my lungs like I had lost my screws. Little did they know that Maribella had barricaded herself inside her home in an attempt to avoid the first day of school. She was afraid of everything and anything new.

Instead of embracing all the new opportunities that were going to come forth this year, she just wanted to stand still in time. As her friend, I could not stand idly by and let her do that.

"Maribella, I have something for you. It's a present for your first day of school."

"What is it?" Her yell was muffled through her front door.

"It's a surprise. If I tell you what it is, then it will take away some of the magic of the gift. Come on, you have to come."

The idea of a gift was so overpowering that Maribella was out the door in less than a minute. She looked *different.* She was already beautiful, but man, the summer did something more. Her eyes were emerald green, and her fur was silky black. Her coat seemed to glisten, even on this overcast day.

"Come. I have something I want to show you," I said, leading her to the opposite side of the road so we could start walking to school. Sometimes I felt it was just best to get started, and Maribella would follow. She didn't enjoy the sight of me leaving her behind, and I knew that would prompt her to start walking.

"I have to tell you something," I said, remembering Johnny's smart remarks in tea-making class.

"So yesterday I noticed that Mrs. Gringalgool's cardigan had a hole in it, and I wanted to fix it. I thought she would appreciate it. You know, being Mrs. Gringalgool, she has a lot going on. So I started sewing her sweater together, and Johnny starts being Johnny again with his sarcastic remarks."

Maribella just listened. She was always so good at that.

"After I finished and handed her the sweater, she was happy about it, and you know, so was I. I know it sounds small, but there is something about fixing and creating that I love, even when it comes down to the needle and thread. Why does Johnny have to be so sarcastic about it? It's like he thinks I shouldn't be doing things like that as a boy. He always has to say something about it."

I think Maribella understood a little bit. We had both lost our parents, so we had to compensate by doing some of the things that they would have done, and it didn't hurt that we loved it. It was just us being us. Maribella, for example, mowed the lawn a lot. She probably did that a lot this summer. She looked fit and definitely more toned.

Maribella let out a deep sigh.

"Alistar … don't let him get to you," she said. "He will just never get it 'cause he's not like us." Although Johnny physically looked like us and shared our genes to some extent, he really didn't get it. He didn't lose a parent. He didn't understand that sometimes we had to fill in for our parents.

"We are almost there."

"Where?" Maribella asked.

I hopped over the fence into Hummingbird Forest, just at the spot I had been yesterday. "Come on. I want to show you something," I said as I walked toward the willow tree. Maribella stood there for a moment with her arms crossed, looking at me with both fear and intrigue in her eyes. It was a look she often gave just as she was about to jump alongside me.

There she goes, I thought. She hopped the fence and caught up to me, and we went off. "I just want to grab some fruit," I told her. I mean, it was partly true because I was going to grab the burnaberries near the willow tree.

Just as I did the other day, I put my backpack down and filled it up with the abundance of fruit that had fallen from the tree.

"Alistar. If you needed lunch money, I could have given you some." Maribella was always insisting that I take from her, and I didn't want to. I was at a point where I wanted to pave my own way.

"Chompers!" I started toward the bush Chompers had jumped out of the other day.

Maribella looked at me, confused.

"Chompers!" I repeated, hoping he would hear me.

"Alistar! Have you gone mad? What are you doing? What is a Chompers?" Maribella began to fill the air with her persistent questions.

"Wait," I said to her as I saw Chompers reappear from the bushes and start making its way toward us. Chompers was walking right outside of Maribella's view. I grabbed both her shoulders and turned her around and pointed her toward Chompers.

"Look!" I said to her, hoping she would see the beauty I saw.

She was intrigued.

"Oh! Where did he come from? It is a he, right?"

"I don't know, Maribella. Whatever *it* is, it's my friend." The raganoo was next to us, and we pet its beak and silky, soft feathers.

"You know, raganoos are one the most protected creatures in Creatopia. It was in Mr. Wendon's class that they were talking about how the Ministry has a special place for them in Hummingbird Forest. It seems like some of the kingdoms have been trying to use them for shows. The Ministry is not very fond of this," Maribella said, looking into the raganoo's peaceful brown eyes.

"Want to see something?"

I picked a few burnaberries off the ground.

"Watch!" I threw three of them up in the air, and Chompers jumped up on his hind legs and quickly smashed all of them in the air, splattering the remnants all over us.

"Alistar! I'm all messy for school now!" Maribella complained in that way she did when she was just trying to get her point across, without an ounce of anger in her voice.

"Okay, let's go now, or we are going to be *late* late."

"Bye, Chompers!" we shouted as we headed back over the fence.

I loved that Maribella loved Chompers as much as I did and that we had this secret together.

As the days went by, Maribella stopped coming to see Chompers. It wasn't a risk she wanted to take—getting caught wandering around the forest. It wasn't a safe place to be with all of the mysterious disappearances taking place. We just hugged, and I watched her go on her way as I continued to hop the fence and play with Chompers.

"Chompers, what's it like to fly?" I asked him one day. He just looked at me with his dopey eyes, unresponsive. It was silly of me to think he would respond to me.

We were gazing up at the gray skies as the clouds moved in. The grass was wet and had begun to seep into my jeans, but I didn't care. I had a new friend now, and he could fly.

"Fly? Is that what you want?" I heard a tiny voice say from near the willow tree. I looked around and didn't see anyone.

"Flying raganoos are one thing, but if you want to really fly, you'll want to sit on a dragonfly," the voice said, now sounding just inches away from me. I looked around frantically. Not a being in sight. I felt something jump on my leg.

"Ahhhh!" looking down and screaming, I kicked it off. Something shiny went flying to the right as the very peculiar creature landed, just a foot away from me.

"A frog? What's this frog doing here?"

"Alistar, my boy," the frog said. "I've been waiting for you."

I picked up my things and jetted toward the fence. The peculiar frog hopped toward the shiny object that had fallen to the ground, took a moment, and placed the object on his head.

CHAPTER 7

The One

For the next few weeks, I avoided Hummingbird Forest. There was already a lot going on in the kingdom, and I could not bear to bring my father any grief. Mr. Wendon had assigned our class a project. We were to create a landscape view of what Creatopia would look like in the future. I wasn't excited about it at first. Mr. Wendon had mentioned a surprise guest coming to visit on presentation day possibly. He wanted us to stick to what the kingdom was used to. I hated that. Everything was so black and white and so uncreative in my mind. I had gone to Mr. Toddly's House of Arts and Crafts to add more to my collection. I needed a huge piece of cardboard for the surface. Each kingdom would be molded with dough and then painted with very vibrant colors. I added glitter for a little sparkle and molded the creatures that resided in Creatopia. There was one thing I found a bit off. The roads did not seem to match what was in the history books. During King Zazar's reign, he had created roads that led to each kingdom, but now they had disappeared. I wanted to show that in my presentation. When I finally finished and looked at my project, I was energized seeing everything come to life. It was a vision, something I created from scratch. First, I imagined the look on Mr. Wendon's face of disappointment for going offtrack, but then I was excited about what was in store for the future.

"You ready to present today?" my father asked as he took the spinach quiche out of the oven and placed a slice on a plate for me. I was hungry, so I grabbed the fork and started stuffing my face as I began to tell my dad about my project.

"Yeah, and I'm pretty excited about it. I've been working on it for weeks. It's kind of unconventional, but I think it could work."

"Let me take a look."

I put down my fork and ran up the steps to my bedroom. It was sitting on my bed, ready to go. I grabbed my project and looked at it once more, thinking, *This is exactly what we need.* I remembered looking through the history books of King Zazar. He didn't seem to fit any of what the royals were like today. He was different—*colorful.*

"Ta-dah!" I said to my dad with excitement.

"Alistar, this is magnificent. You did this?"

"Yeah! I went to Toddly's just to grab a few things. Very little because I had almost everything already, but yeah ... this is all me," I said, smiling.

"This is absolutely beautiful," my father repeated as he began to take out his camera to take some photos of me standing next to my project.

"Stand there," he said, guiding me to stand right in front of my project. I don't know how to describe it. My project made me feel more alive than ever. I had created something, and I knew deep down this was what the kingdoms were meant to look like.

"Well, he did say don't go too crazy, but I couldn't help myself."

"Oh shoot. I'm running late. Let's get going."

On our drive, my dad turned on the local radio station. It was another advertisement for King Tia's jars of honey. That commercial went on for hours. The sky was gray, and the clouds started to settle in.

"Looks like it's gonna rain," Dad said as he turned off the radio.

I was hoping it wouldn't rain on my project before I got to Mr. Wendon's class. Maribella didn't want to turn in her project. She kept going on and on about how she didn't want to stand in front of the class and present. Maribella was something else. How could she get through life if everything scared her? She did have fun with Chompers, but it was short-lived. She didn't want to go back again and was lost in her thoughts of trouble.

"There he is again!" I shouted in the car, making my father jolt backward and stomp on the brakes.

"My project!" I looked back, and some of the creatures looked a little out of place, but I could still fix it. I had my emergency glue in my backpack. I looked back toward the fence again.

"Alistar, is everything all right?" My father asked, waiting for me to respond to the chaotic stopping of the vehicle.

"Yeah, Dad … uh, sorry … I … ah … thought I saw something."

I looked back at the fence. He had gone. The frog with the shiny object was sitting there, staring at our car like he had something to tell me.

We pulled up in front of the school, and I scurried to drop off my project in Mr. Wendon's class. Mrs. Gringalgool was waiting for me at the door when I arrived.

"Late again, I see," she said, smiling. Ever since I fixed her cardigan, she'd been going easier on me for my tardiness.

"Yeah, I'm sorry. I had to drop off my project at Mr. Wendon's class."

During class, Mrs. Gringalgool kept going on and on about the benefits of ginger tea. She had dried up some ginger root and tea leaves and had us using a pestle and mortar to mix it. I couldn't focus. I kept thinking about the drive to school with Dad and the frog I saw looking back at me as he sat on the fence. What did he want, and how did he know my name?

The very thought of a stranger knowing my name freaked me out.

"Alistar, are you okay?"

The bell had rung, and I was the only student left in the classroom. Mrs. Gringalgool was picking up her things to head out the door. The fresh smell of ginger helped to awaken my senses again.

"Yes, I'm okay … just thinking," I said while I was packing my bag to go to Mr. Wendon's class.

She was drinking what seemed to be a carton of milk and going on and on about how she had parent-teacher conferences to attend all afternoon.

There was something written on the carton of milk she was drinking. *King missing*, it read. She moved her paw out of the way, and I couldn't believe my eyes. The frog I had seen was him!

"Mrs. Gringalgool, who is that?" I asked.

She turned the carton around and looked at me in disbelief.

"You really need to turn on the news, Alistar," Mrs. Gringalgool said in sadness.

"This is King Hently of Palace Pond, and there are search teams looking for him all over Creatopia. He's been missing for months."

CHAPTER 8
Glittering Hope

I tried to wrap my head around what Mrs. Gringalgool had just told me. The thought of a king who was missing and wanted to speak to me was something I couldn't quite fathom.

Sitting in Mr. Wendon's class, hearing him do roll call seemed so normal for such an abnormal day. It was presentation day, and Maribella had already started her anxiety routine. She was tapping her feet on the ground and scribbling in her notebook. She told me once that she scribbled because it helped her calm down. I tried it once, but it didn't work for me. I didn't like how the gray tip of the pencil hit my college-ruled paper. I preferred to sketch with colored pencils. That really spoke to me, seeing the different colors drift across the paper. When I pressed the color pencils just hard enough, it would leave a small indent in the white paper. *I left my mark*, I would think. This is what lit me up. I was so excited to be able to finally present my work to Mr. Wendon. There wasn't a lot of room for creativity at Vennister High School. We mainly focused on classes that spoke about the history of our nation and classes that would help us become something that was of use to the kingdom. For example, there was a welding class. King Tia believed in the importance of having sharp tools that were ready for battle. He wanted to make sure we were always fully stocked and most of our funds for anything creative usually went to the classes that promoted welding.

There were some after-school activities that focused on the arts but not many. King Tia didn't want that spreading around the kingdom. It wasn't useful, I guess.

"Alistar ... can you help me?" asked Maribella, batting her eyelashes.

"What do you need help with?" I responded.

"Well, for part of my project, I don't know what to do. I bought green construction paper for the grass, and I cut up this little piece and laid them flat, but it looks like it needs more."

"Let me take a look," I offered. Maribella needed a little bit of sparkle. I knew she wanted her project to pop out.

"Maribella, this is absolutely beautiful. If I could make one suggestion, if you have the time, I would try to make the grass stand up instead of lay flat. That will add dimension to your project. Here, I'll help you." We started to bunch up the little pieces of grass together, tie them with rubber bands, and stick them up with glue underneath.

"See, this adds depth," I pointed out.

Maribella looked at her project with excitement as I heard Mr. Wendon make his announcement.

"Today, class is special. We have a guest who will be joining us. When he heard about our presentations, he insisted on being part of the class. I want you guys to be on your absolute best behavior."

Maribella popped another mint in her mouth as Mr. Wendon spoke.

"King Tia will be joining us in just a few moments."

She wasn't ready for that. It was one thing for her to have prepared for this presentation, but now the king of Carrot Kingdom was going to join us?

I scanned the class for their reactions and found that Johnny Jester seemed unbothered. He was puffing out his chest more than usual. His dad ran the local Carrot Kingdom newspaper and was always putting King Tia in good light. So Johnny had an edge over most of us. It didn't hurt him either that his dad was always helping place King Tia's honey farm advertisements on the front page. Another way to get close with the in crowd, I guess.

Johnny's project looked a bit plain to me. All black and white from what I could see. He had his little army figures plastered everywhere, and I didn't see any of the other kingdoms in sight. It was probably going to get an A++ from King Tia, since he was always all about his own kingdom and his *army*. Johnny looked back in my direction, smirking and whispering to one of his goons next to him. They both chuckled at Maribella and walked toward us.

"What do you have there Alis-girl?" Johnny mocked. He lifted the white cloth I had draped over my project and began to examine it closely. "All that glitter. It's hurting my eyes. Did you get it from your mom's closet?" It was just like Johnny to hit below the belt. He knew my mother had passed, yet he would bring her up from time to time just to add insult to injury. *Not today,* I thought. I was done with Johnny and his dumb remarks. I felt my blood boil. Maribella squeezed my hand under the table, as she often did when she could sense I was getting angry. *Three deep breaths,* I thought.

Mr. Wendon walked over to see what the commotion was about. "Everything okay here?" he asked.

"Yes, Mr. Wendon," all three of us replied like drones. It was always an uphill battle with Johnny, and I grew tired of trying to fight the good fight.

"Alistar, your project looks so good. I really like how you put the glitter in the rivers and ponds. It really makes it pop," Johnny said.

"That is such a nice thing to say, Johnny. What do you say, Alistar?" Mr. Wendon pushed. Was Mr. Wendon kidding or what? Johnny was the problem and his simple black-and-white project. I was done being nice.

"Mr. Wendon ..." I began to say.

"Hold on, Alistar." Mr. Wendon's attention went toward the classroom door.

"Everybody, rise," Mr. Wendon prompted as King Tia arrived. The class stood up as he walked into the classroom with his entourage. Up close, King Tia looked short, not like my dad's photos embellished him in size. He had brown, matted fur and deep hazel eyes. He wore a very impressive red velvet suit, which I'm sure someone worked day and night to perfect, as we knew he was picky about his appearance. He had the most elaborate crown on, one that I couldn't even dream up. It had three tiers and held colorful stones that seemed to add the glamour that I loved so dearly.

"Hello, everyone!" he said to the class.

"Hello, King Tia," the class responded. Mr. Wendon looked around the class to make sure everyone was on their best behavior.

"I have come here today because a little birdy told me this class was working on something special, real special. I don't know what Mr. Wendon told you about what we want to do with your project, but we are always looking for talent to bring into our castle. I'm looking for a special boy or girl to bring onto our team to help make Carrot Kingdom one of the best places to live and work. A selected one of you will be offered a full college scholarship and a place to work once you've graduated, here in Carrot Kingdom, our creative community that pushes on making real changes in our kingdom."

I started to feel butterflies of excitement in my belly. I was already excited that I would be able to present my project, but now King Tia was here offering us a free ride for college and a place to work in the creative sector—a place with the royals where I could bring real change.

My dad walked into the classroom with his suitcase and camera gear, ready to take photos. I had never seen him in action at work before. He looked different to me. He looked *drained*. My dad spotted me from the front of the classroom and gave me a half-crooked smile. *Something doesn't feel right,* I thought.

The students laid out their projects on the table as King Tia came by to inspect. I saw him pass Johnny Jester's and give him a slight smile with a thumbs-up. I knew he would be attracted to Johnny's, but I still had hope. You never knew with King Tia.

"My, my, what do we have here?" King Tia came by and looked at Maribella's project. Maribella had left her seat and run to the bathroom. The feeling of anxiety had consumed her once again.

"That's Maribella's," I chimed in. "She really wanted to emphasize the importance of conserving the plants and trees. So she dove deep into that part of Creatopia."

"And who are you?" King Tia said, turning in my direction.

"My name is Alistar Sparks."

"Sparks, Sparks, Sparks. Where have I heard that name before?"

"My dad. He works for you and is right over there."

King Tia turned and looked at my father in disgust. "Oh, he's your father?"

"Yeah."

Humph. He let out a sigh of disapproval.

Something didn't feel quite right. King Tia began deconstructing my project.

"What's that supposed to be?" he inquired.

He was now paying attention to the roads I had created to connect the kingdoms together.

"That's the roads, Your Highness."

Hmph. "Why are you adding roads to Creatopia that lead to the other kingdoms? We are not part of *those* kingdoms. Do you not like your own Carrot Kingdom?"

"I just did some research and saw that they were connected during King Zazar's reign."

The room fell silent, as I had just said the one thing that could make King Tia fall into a fury.

"We don't have roads to the other kingdoms!" King Tia shouted. "This is absolutely unnecessary, and I don't want this being brought up in my kingdom's schools. We move through the nation alone. The other kingdoms are not for us to worry about, as they do not worry about us. Do you understand, Alistar?"

I felt confused about where all this anger was coming from. I looked at my father, who nervously nodded for me to nod along.

"Yes, Your Highness."

"Mr. Wendon, get rid of it. I don't know what's being taught here, but we must learn to stand alone, strong and tall, not with the help or connection to the other kingdoms. They are nothing to us. You see this?" he said, pointing at Johnny's project. "This is what I'm looking for. This is power. It tells a story that I want our kingdom to be about. Yours," he said as he pointed to my project, "is for the girls and boys that do not show real strength. The weak-minded," he said, tapping his large, brown, furry finger on my project and looking at me with rage.

Mr. Wendon came to my side and covered up my project.

"Everyone, may I have your attention?" King Tia was now directing the class to look in my direction. "I want you to look at this project for a moment. Look at what Alistar created." The class began to murmur as I looked around the room. Mr. Wendon gave me a crooked smile when I made eye contact with him.

"Can anyone tell me what's wrong?" I could see Johnny grinning ear from ear as I stood there horrified by what was taking place.

"No one? Okay. Let me educate you all here today. I'm almost glad I came across Alistar's project." The king continued to speak, and I could feel my heart drop to the pit of my stomach as he glared at me and then back at the students, who now seemed to be intensely focused on my project.

"The first thing I want you to note is that Alistar did not follow directions. He was to create the kingdom in a light that shows the progression with the rules being followed now. We want higher walls that separate us from the others and more military to fight those who choose to challenge us. We want a strong kingdom, and a project where we dance and unite with the other kingdoms leads to a life of being vulnerable. We don't want that, do we?"

The class nodded along like drones.

"Alistar, can you tell me where King Zazar is now?"

"He's gone, sir," I responded.

"What happened to all his ideas and unity of the creatures?" I knew the answer to this but had a hard time saying that everyone went their separate ways.

"Now, class, there was a time where a king once existed. He went by the name King Zazar, a colorful lemur that thought uniting all from sea, land, and air would do the nation great justice, but what he failed to realize is that ideas and creativity and unity don't lead to success. The world isn't as colorful as we hope it to be. We must rely on our military and our strength to protect us. To be creative and dream of a nation of glitter and sparkle just seems weak and childish. When King Zazar passed, so did the idea of unity and a colorful kingdom filled with beauty. It doesn't help us. We don't need the others. We are making more money now, and our kingdom is growing. We have one of the best armies in all of Creatopia." King Tia stopped speaking and looked around the classroom. I could see some of the other students had covered their projects up.

"Do you understand? We must all follow what *this* kingdom is about and not the others. Even a mere project showcasing what you've showcased tells me where your mind is at, and I want it out of there." King Tia looked taller than he did when he walked in. He was filled with so much anger, and I wasn't sure where it had all come from.

"Mr. Wendon, I'll have a talk with you later," King Tia said, walking out the classroom door. My dad gave me an awkward smile and followed right behind him in a hurry. I didn't blame my dad for leaving without a proper goodbye. This was our bread and butter and apparently how the kingdom worked.

I felt a bit dazed. I wasn't sure what to think as I started to deconstruct my project. It was painful to take the pieces apart and throw them in the trash. The glitter fell to the ground as I started to break it apart. Maribella was nowhere in sight, and Johnny's chest looked like it was going to burst out of his shirt. I was sure he was getting so much pleasure out of seeing that the king didn't feel I was a fit.

"Bye, Alis-girl," Johnny said, walking out the door as the bell rang to signal the end of last period.

I just sat in my chair for a moment, waiting for Maribella to come back from the bathroom.

"I'm sorry, Alistar. I should have checked everyone's project. This is my fault," Mr. Wendon said as he sat next to me. "I know that you worked really hard on that, and although I appreciated it, it's just not what this kingdom needs." I could hear the words Mr. Wendon was saying, but I refused to believe them. It was like everyone was drones or something.

"I get it, Mr. Wendon. I'm not going to be everyone's cup of tea."

Mr. Wendon started to go on and on about the kingdoms and the feuds that were going on. He wanted me to know it wasn't my fault that sometimes King Tia lost his temper. He was just stressed. I couldn't help but think of the words of King Hently in Hummingbird Forest. "If you really want to fly, you'll want to sit on a dragonfly."

CHAPTER 9
Premonition

I opened my eyes to the sunlight and clear blue skies. The clouds were just moving in, and the warm breeze felt comforting against my fur. The rolling hills rose to new heights that I'd never seen before. I was outside on what looked to be a giant sunflower. Lying on my back, the warmth of the sunlight embraced me. I could hear the buzzing sound in the distance getting closer. King Hently glided down from the sky on a giant dragonfly and landed next to me. "Come on, Alistar," he encouraged. "If you really want to fly, you'll want to sit on a dragonfly."

Beep. Beep. Beep.

It was the first day of winter vacation, and school was out. I moved my arm around the nightstand and clicked the snooze button.

"Alistar, are you awake?" My dad came barging in the room. I pulled the sheets above my ears. After the whole class presentation debacle, I was not in a good place. I felt so drained from trying to always do everything so extravagant and sparkly. It was clear that the kingdom did not need it. We had started our winter vacation, and I vowed to sleep in every day until school came back around.

"Dad, I want to sleep in today," I said, yawning. I could see that something was not right. My dad looked anxious.

"Come downstairs. There is something going on at Carrot Kingdom. They are saying he is *gone*." My mind flooded with thoughts of who it might be. *Another guard, I suppose. He's not gone; he probably ran away like the rest of King Tia's men. He's just awful to work with.*

We both sat down in the living room as my dad looked around our tan, corduroy sofa for our remote. A news reporter appeared on the screen.

"Story still developing at this time, but we are right outside the home of King Tia's castle. It appears that, in the night, King Tia disappeared. He has gone missing, just eight months after the disappearance of King Hently. What we found in his bedroom was a watch that may have been dropped and a missing bedsheet. The castle's security team is urging

anyone with information about the disappearance to come forward."
King Tia has gone missing? How? I thought. He had one of the best
armies in Creatopia.

"They are saying that they can't point out anything malicious,
which is a good thing. I can't imagine what his family is going through
at this time." As my father continued to speak, guilt began to settle in.
I knew where King Hently was. Why hadn't I told my father about the
mysterious spotting of King Hently in Hummingbird Forest? I knew
I wasn't supposed to be there, but would he understand that I was just
trying to pick up berries before school? I didn't want to go hungry. Dad
was always trying to make sure I stayed on the path, and there I was,
messing things up for him. If anyone found out that I knew where King
Hently was and didn't say anything, I would be looked at as a suspect,
and Dad could get in a lot of trouble. The kingdom didn't take kindly
to secrecy like that.

"There is a town hall meeting tonight," my dad said as the news
drifted into another commercial about a sale at King Tia's honey farm.

"We are going to go tonight. Mrs. Stagger called earlier and asked
if we could take Maribella to the meeting, as she is flooded with work
since King Tia's disappearance."

"I'll go pick her up!" I nearly shouted. I needed to see Maribella. As
anxious as she was, she could help me.

"Are you sure? We can go together in my truck. It's cold out."

"Yeah, Dad. I'm sure. I just feel like going on a walk."

"Okay, be back soon, and, Alistar! Stay on the path. I don't want
anything happening to you."

"I will, Dad. I love you," I said. I exited through the kitchen door
and went onto Redwood Road.

The air felt crisp and breezy against my nose. What in the world was
happening? Why had King Hently and now King Tia gone missing? I
walked toward Maribella's home, fixated on figuring out a way to tell
Dad that I didn't stay on path.

Knock, knock, knock.

"Maribella, I need to talk to you."

Knock, knock, knock.

"Maribella, open up. It's important," I pleaded.

I saw Maribella peak out through her living room window. She finally opened the door.

"All right, come in," she grumbled. Maribella was not a morning person. Even for her, this was too early.

"Did you see the news?"

"Yeah," she said, putting four pieces of toast in the toaster. She made two cups of Earl Grey tea, and we sat down at the kitchen table. Her home was much bigger than mine, and her mom was always remodeling their home. They had soft gray walls and white crown molding. Maribella's mom really liked her emerald-green marble countertops. I remember Maribella telling me that one time in the store, her mom went through every aisle looking for the perfect color. Maribella said she was always patient with her mom when she got into things like remodeling the house. She knew it was hard without her dad there, and it seemed to cheer up her mom.

"*Mmmm.* Thank you for the tea," I said, trying to ease myself into saying what I was going to say next, without having Maribella go into the anxiety box.

"Maribella, I have to tell you something. I know this is going to sound crazy, but I want you to listen."

"I'm listening," Maribella said as she flipped through her latest issue of *Teen Girl* magazine.

"I saw him—the missing king."

"Yeah, we all saw him, Alistar. What's your point?"

"No, I saw King Hently. I know where he is."

Maribella was eating a piece of toast at the time, and it fell out of her mouth and landed in her tea.

"Remember when we hugged at our spot near Redwood Road

before I hopped the fence? You went to school, and I went to go see Chompers? I was lying on the grass when I heard a small voice from the bushes. I looked around and saw a frog talking to me. I got scared and ran toward the school. When I got to Mrs. Gringalgool's class, I found out that he was missing too." I paused because what I was going to say next would either entice Maribella or force her into her anxiety box.

"Maribella, we need to go back to the woods and help the king come back. He may know where King Tia is."

Maribella seemed eerily calm. I wondered what she was thinking. Whenever she got quiet, it reminded me of the time when I convinced her to save a beached narwhal. We were on a trip to Narwhal Landing with Dad and Mrs. Staggers when I spotted a narwhal stuck on the beach. "Come on, Maribella. Let's go!" I prompted, trying to get her closer to the narwhal. I could see that it was struggling to get back into the ocean. Dad and Mrs. Staggers just watched us as we walked toward the narwhal. The marine animals were known to be peaceful creatures. I guess they trusted that it wouldn't hurt us.

"I don't know, Alistar. It has a horn. It could hurt us," Maribella said, standing a few feet away. I couldn't wait for Maribella to come around. The narwhal looked like it was in pain.

"I'm not going to hurt you," I said to the narwhal and started to push it back into the ocean. Every fiber of my being was being tested. I couldn't budge the narwhal an inch. "Maribella, I need you! The narwhal is stuck and could die out here." Dad and Mrs. Staggers started to walk toward Maribella and me. They may have been trying to teach us something. Maribella jumped in and began to push. Slowly, we were able to move the narwhal closer to the ocean, and it began to swim.

"Thank you!" it said as it swam away. That was the day that I knew Maribella would come through if it meant saving another.

Knock, knock, knock.

"Are you expecting someone?" I asked Maribella.

"No. I wonder who that could be." Maribella got up from the kitchen table and walked over to look out the window.

"Alistar! It's your dad." As she opened the door, she said, "Hello, Mr. Sparks."

"Dad, I thought you were going to stay home. We were just getting ready to walk back home."

"It's okay, Alistar. The town hall meeting is starting fairly soon. We have got to get going. This isn't one of those meetings we can miss."

When we entered Carrot Kingdom, it was not as I had remembered it as a young boy when Dad would bring me to work. The guards didn't even check our identification to see if we were who we said we were. Many of the shops in the shopping center said *closing* or *out of business*. What was happening?

"Lilly's ice-cream shop!" I exclaimed as we passed it. I remembered as a kid walking in that shop with my dad, and we would get the sherbet ice cream; it was one of my favorites on a hot summer day. We parked near the shop, and I ran out of the car. I wanted to say hello to Mr. Monti, the owner of Lilly's ice-cream shop.

"Hello, Mr. Monti," I said, looking around the shop. Mr. Monti was an older rabbit. He walked out with his cane and half-moon-shaped glasses. He was always a very classy man, as I remembered, wearing suits to work with the tweed elbow patches. It inspired me as a kid to start sewing tweed on my long-sleeve shirts. I really liked the look that he had going on.

"Alistar, is that you?" It was amazing how he remembered me. It had been at least seven years since I had seen him. King Tia really enforced rules about outsiders visiting the kingdom. Since Dad and I weren't part of the kingdom community, as Dad only worked there, we weren't really allowed to go in. King Tia believed that rich and poor should live separately. It was all about status to him and showing the kingdom that he was powerful through money. Dad didn't seem to mind King Tia's rude remarks from time to time. He often criticized my dad for working at home rather than staying late in the kingdom to finish up his work.

"Yes, it's me! It's been so long since I've seen you! How is Lilly?"

"Lilly is doing great and is attending the private school here. She got a job in the castle working in the kitchen for now. She hopes to work her way up to the chef role."

Mr. Monti didn't look like himself. He wasn't wearing his suit and his colorful shirts anymore. The store used to be a lavender pink with lots of artwork on the wall. The flavors were his creations. I remember trying a lemon ricotta flavor that he had just created. That one was very popular, but today, as I looked at him, much had changed since I was last there. He was wearing a uniform, and even the flavors of the ice cream had changed. Much of what made Lilly's ice-cream shop, his impeccable suits and unique flavors, had been erased.

"Hey, Mr. Monti. What is the flavor of the month?" I inquired.

"Oh, no, Alistar. We stopped doing that a few years ago."

"Why?" I pressed. Why would Mr. Monti stop doing what made him *him*?

"Alistar, we have to get going soon," my dad said, coming into the store to remind me we had to head over to town hall.

"I'll be out in just a second, Dad."

"Sorry, Mr. Monti. What happened?"

"Well, one day King Tia walked in after a long day. I was getting ready to close up shop when he wanted to try one of my creations. I had worked on this cherry combination that had chocolate and sprinkles and whipped cream. He gave it a try, and I could tell he didn't like it very much. He knew I had a daughter who one day wanted to work in the castle, so he advised me to make the flavors 'more traditional,' as he called it, and he would consider letting her work in the kitchen and working her way up. King Tia is a very straightforward man. He knows what he likes, and there is no changing his mind."

Boy, did I know what Mr. Monti was talking about, remembering the class project fiasco and the glitter on my project. I hadn't realized, however, that it had become a *thing* everywhere.

"Well, I remember your lemon ricotta ice cream. I hope you bring that back. It was my favorite."

There was a glimmer of happiness is Mr. Monti's eyes as I said that and waved goodbye to head off to town hall with Dad and Maribella.

CHAPTER 10

A Lost Queen

The doors opened to the town hall, and everyone shuffled in. You could tell who lived at Carrot Kingdom and who belonged to the outskirts, like Maribella and I. Johnny was up front with his dad, standing next to Queen Penelope. Johnny's dad, although he lived in the outskirts, seemed to have formed relationships with the royals.

Queen Penelope was one of the most beautiful creatures I had ever seen. She was different up close than what I'd seen on TV. Her gray fur looked silky from afar, and she had striking, dark hazel eyes. She wore a velvet yellow dress with ruby-red stones. Her crown, like King Tia's, had three tiers with sparkly stones of red, green, yellow, and blue. She wore a long, red velvet dress with a gold lace trim that reached the stage floor.

"Today, I bring to you a day of great sadness for the kingdom." When Queen Penelope spoke, there was dead silence in the hall. It was customary when a royal spoke to stop and pay attention intently. To do anything less would be seen as a sign of disrespect. Not even the shuffling of one's feet could be heard.

"We have search teams all throughout the kingdom and

Hummingbird Forest looking for the king, and no sign of him has been found. King Tia and I have been together for twenty-five years, and my heart tells me he is still out there. This much I know. I urge anyone with information to come forward." Queen Penelope stepped away from the microphone for a moment. I couldn't imagine that losing the one you loved dearly, without a sign of them, would be easy. It was the not knowing that appeared to hurt her the most. Johnny Jester's father reached into his coat pocket and provided a tissue for Queen Penelope's tears. After a moment of collecting herself, she stepped back toward the microphone.

"For anyone who can bring me back my husband, he shall be crowned the next king of Carrot Kingdom." The crowd broke out of the silence. This was an unlikely route for the kingdom to take—to just give *anyone* the crown.

"Silence, silence!" one of the guards shouted.

The excitement in the crowd became electric throughout the room.

"Mom, I could be king," a little girl whispered next to me. The mom smiled as she looked at her daughter's excitement.

"I just want my husband back. Since we do not have any children of our own at this time to pass the crown along to, it shall be passed along to the one who can solve the greatest tragedy to reverberate throughout our kingdom."

Maribella began to nudge me. "Alistar, is there anything you want to say?" I ignored Maribella. I didn't believe it was the time to say anything.

"*Shhh*, you two." My dad looked at Maribella and me and pleaded with his eyes for us to be quiet. Technically, we were both at his worksite, although King Tia was nowhere to be seen, and he wanted us to be on our best behavior.

After the town hall meeting ended, we all went to say goodbye to Mr. Monti at Lilly's ice-cream shop, but he had already gone.

The kingdom seemed like a ghost town—not what I had imagined Carrot Kingdom to look like at night.

"Dad, where is everybody?" I asked.

"There is a curfew here. Everyone needs to be in their homes with the lights off, or they will be fined."

I thought that to be an odd rule. I guess when you have a place of power, rules become something to play with.

My mind drifted into what Carrot Kingdom would look like if I were king. Everyone would have a raganoo. Raganoos would be part our kingdom and would be family. We would have giant feast nights where we all shared and brought our favorite dishes. I would implement a creativity plan where everyone went a little crazy and creative with what they wanted the kingdom to look and feel like. *It's their home too*, I thought. *They should feel like it.*

My castle would be colorful, and I would want to get to know the other kingdoms and towns around. Everyone would be welcome.

I didn't even notice that Johnny and his dad were walking behind us as we reached my dad's truck.

"Oh, hello there, David. I didn't see you there."

"Hi, Jed. How's the photography business going?"

"Well, it looks like I'll be out of work for a bit, since King Tia is missing."

I hadn't even thought of that. What would happen to Dad's job? How were we going to survive?

"Well, if you need any work, I know a few people. Just give me a call."

That was really nice of Johnny's dad.

"Alistar."

Oh, boy. Here we go.

"Are you going to go look for this king?" Johnny asked in that way he always asked to get under my skin. I always felt like he was picking on me. It was hard for me to tell when he wasn't. I had been pushed around by him way too many times.

"I might," I answered very shortly. I knew it was best to say less to Johnny. That way, he didn't have much to use in order to pick on me.

My dad began to look at me with his side-eye and was silently telling me that I would have no part in the search. He was probably right; it would be too dangerous for me to go.

"Well … you know there is a girls' team and boys' team forming. My sister, Jenny, would love to have you on her team. I told her about your little art show." And there it was. The icing on the carrot cake for me. He thought I was a girl because I liked glitter and was interested in fashion. I hated that about Johnny.

"Come on, kids." My dad urged us into the truck.

On our drive home, I could feel my blood boiling from Johnny's remarks. It had been like that all my life. I was always looked at differently because I was a boy rabbit who liked the arts. It was as though I didn't have any power because no one saw my art as useful. Even from the king's mouth, my creativity was too much for his kingdom.

I could feel Maribella squeeze my hand in the car as we drove home. Maribella got it. There were so many days where we talked about our projects and bringing our ideas to life, and in those moments, I felt most alive. The love of art seemed to fill the gap I felt in my heart.

CHAPTER 11

Slumber Party

In my dimly lit room, I looked at the narwhals plastered all over the wall. I remember outlining the narwhals with glow in the dark paint so when nighttime fell I wouldn't be all alone. They would glow on the walls and offer me a sense of comfort in the absence of Dad or Maribella. I couldn't sleep after the town hall meeting. Something sparked inside me after I heard that they were going to give the throne to just *anybody*. *Why not me?* I knew that in the eyes of King Tia, I wasn't someone who could lead the kingdom. My view and talents were not what they needed. Ever since King Zazar appointed the original royals to their thrones, the crowns remained in the family. How could I, Alistar Sparks, ever be able to step into the role of king? I seemed so ill-fitted for anything they were looking for. I wasn't strong. How could I withstand a beast in the midst of a duel if I couldn't run quickly? Every year, I tried to make it before the seven-minute mark on the one-mile run but couldn't. Johnny could though. He was one of the fastest kids in school. He excelled in all of our PE classes, and I was sure if he was faced with a beast, he could easily slay his enemy. I wished I had listened more to what my counselor told me about taking more physical education classes. Then I would be in a position to search for the king.

I was swarmed with thoughts of defeat when I remembered something Dad said about Mom whenever she became upset. Dad always said that Mom would go into her hobby of knitting whenever she was sad, and with each movement, she would knit up creations that would turn heads around the town. It was her magic fuel, Dad would say. Mom would step into her studio, and that seemed to light a fire in her to get out her best work. Now that was what Maribella needed, some magic fuel, and I could sure use some too. I missed Mom. I always thought life would be so much more different if she were here. All I have of hers are the things she left behind. I reached along the side of my bed and dug my hand into my backpack that I had laid on the ground right next to me. *I know it's here somewhere.* I pulled out the lime-green envelope that Dad had given to me on my thirteenth birthday. I usually never read Mom's birthday cards right away. I just wanted to savor the moments we had together. So I had tucked this gem away for a day like this.

"No, Mommy! No, no, no!" Maribella was asleep on the ground in my bedroom. Her mom had to work late and asked if she could stay with us for the weekend. She was muttering in her sleep about saying no to her mom. I guess her daymares had translated into nightmares, and she was caught in her anxiety box while she slept as well. She looked so peaceful as she slept in a slew of blankets my dad had collected from around the house for her. I didn't know anyone who wore a nightcap to bed, but there she was, with her pink, fuzzy nightgown covered in moons and clouds and a nightcap.

Since childhood, she had had a stuffed caterpillar, which she held tightly to her chest. Dad gave her that toy one year for Christmas when she turned seven years old. Maribella's dad died in the winter. I remember when Dad came to our Christmas party at school and brought Maribella the caterpillar. News of her father's death spread through the city like wildfire. Maribella's mom received the news when she was reporting a story live on camera about a house fire. It was one of those things you never want to remind others about. Maribella was probably too young to understand at the time. When Dad dropped off the toy, it was something that connected Maribella and I.

Since that day, we were joined at the hip, and she and I were going to get through our toughest days together. I would never wish for Maribella's dad to die, but in some weird way, I was glad that we were together. She was the missing puzzle piece to my life. I opened up the lime-green envelope and pulled out the letter. It was on a clean sheet of white paper, although you could tell that some time had slipped into the letter. The paper didn't feel new, like the feeling I got ripping open the plastic from a fresh batch of construction paper. No, this felt ... different.

Dear Alistar,

Happy birthday! I hope your year has been filled with surprise, magic, and mystery. I know this isn't how you want to spend your birthday, and trust me, I wish I was there to celebrate it with you. If I know your father, he probably made you a batch of his famous birthday pancakes. He probably won't tell you though that he is using my secret recipe.

This made me smile, thinking back to the day of my birthday and smelling the pancakes. *It was all Mom,* I thought. She did spend that day with us in a way. My heart quickly faded into feeling heaviness. That was why I always waited to open the letter. It was like a double-edged sword. It would serve to bring me joy just for a moment, and then I would remember she was gone.

The hallway light went on. *Dad must be awake*, I thought. I quickly tucked the letter in my backpack and closed my eyes.

"Alistar, you awake?" my dad said, tiptoeing into the room. I kept my eyes closed. I didn't know why I did it. I guess I just wanted to see if he would try a little harder to wake me up.

"Alistar, I thought I heard you," my dad prompted. He was right next to me.

"Alistar?" he again prompted. I could sense he was going to go full-throttle tickling me if I didn't wake up or show some sign of existence.

"Dad ... what?" I said, pretending to be half-asleep.

"I have to go into work. Queen Penelope said she needs me there to continue photographing, even though King Tia is gone. Will you and Maribella be okay?"

"Yes," I muttered. Maribella and I were about to have the whole house to ourselves. That meant plenty of jumping on the bed and from sofa to sofa, playing lava. It was a game we made up when we were kids. The ground was hot, molting lava, and the sofa was our safe spot. We had to get around the house without touching the ground at all. We would also probably watch one of those R-rated movies that Dad was always so careful about keeping us from watching.

"There are breakfast burritos in the fridge. I just made some for you guys. I should be home by lunchtime. You can call the castle if you need anything."

I think my dad knew I was excited, although he pretended to ignore it. He kissed me on the forehead and headed out my bedroom door. A few moments later, I heard the kitchen door shut. We had the whole house to ourselves.

CHAPTER 12

Full Circle

I could see his shadow in the darkness. He was quite large. Sitting on his throne of sticks and stones, he dared me to answer. I couldn't say a word or move. He was near me, and that's all I knew—but where?

I felt someone poking my side. I must have fallen back asleep because when I opened my eyes, Maribella was staring at me, holding her stuffed caterpillar. I guess Dad forgot to turn on the heater. The air felt icy inside our home. I could feel the cold air settle on my wet nose. Maribella, still wrapped in a bundle of blankets, hopped on the bed next to me.

"I'm hungry and cold," Maribella said, hinting for me to get up and do something about it.

"Hm ... imagine that," I said to her, drawing my fuzzy sheets back over my face. I wasn't ready to get up just yet.

"Alistar ... I'm hungry."

"Dad left breakfast burritos in the fridge. You're welcome to help yourself to some if you like."

Maribella, now lying right next to me, curled up facing the closet doors and let out a huge sigh. I knew what that meant. She didn't want to go get the breakfast burritos.

"Alistar …"

"Okay, okay. Give me one second, and I'll be right down. Why don't you go down and turn something on for us to watch, and I'll get breakfast ready."

Maribella hopped downstairs, now singing a different tune. I knew she was anxious about going through our fridge. She was all about attending to and respecting boundaries. She meant well, but come *on*, Maribella. You're not robbing the castle. You're just getting breakfast burritos out of the fridge. I put on my robe and headed down the stairs.

I sat on the couch next to Maribella and handed her the burrito. Dad had made eggs with spinach, tomatoes, onions, and bell peppers, all wrapped in lettuce. Maribella's mom was on TV, reviewing last night's town hall meeting. It always amazed me to see Mrs. Stagger on the news. She was so professional in how she dressed, spoke, and carried herself. Although not as captivating in person, she did have a certain movie-star quality about her on TV. Maribella had sunk her teeth into the burrito, and the juices were dripping down on our corduroy sofa.

"Maribella, turn up the volume." A picture of a raganoo had appeared on the screen.

"In breaking news, this is the third raganoo we have found in critical condition, likely due to our current weather conditions, some of the coldest temperatures we've seen in a while. The castle has not opened up an emergency facility to house the raganoos, and without King Tia, they may not. The castle is urging citizens not to go into Hummingbird Forest to try to save the raganoos at this time. They have found that raganoos can turn quite vicious when the cold weather sets in."

"Alistar, what about Chompers?" she said, lowering the volume on the television. Although Maribella showed a mix of anxiety and courage when it came to saving creatures, Maribella stood with courage.

"I have lots of scarves that I knitted and plenty of blankets. Let's go and give them to Chompers."

My mind began to wonder about Chompers, the most beautiful raganoo I had ever seen. He was my friend in the cold and possibly dying. The more I thought about it, the more I felt like I had to do something. Maribella and I bundled up in layers and headed out the kitchen door.

I felt a sharp sting against my nose as the cold morning air wrapped itself around Maribella and me as we stepped out of my toasty home, leaving the smell of coffee and breakfast burritos behind. It woke me up more than Mrs. Gringalgool's snappy ginger tea ever could. Maribella and I were heading out on an adventure, and she was all about it. We walked along the snowy sidewalk of Redwood Road, following the bend of Hummingbird Forest. The snow sat gently on the tree branches, almost heavenly. The sun was bright and shining, although not enough to melt away the snow, just enough to make me feel like I wasn't alone. The funny thing about Hummingbird Forest was that they named it after the hummingbirds. There used to be a whole lot of them. I remember going with Dad just to catch a glimpse of them in the morning.

"Look, Alistar," Dad said to me one day when we were walking through the forest. "There are three of them crowding around that flower. Do you see them? There was a bright purple flower sitting on a leafy green bush, and three of the hummingbirds were pink, yellow, and green, all drinking the sweet nectar the flower offered.

"This is their home," my dad said, gazing at the hummingbirds. He was building his portfolio at the time. For a short moment, he worked as a nature photographer, catching all the creatures in their home environments. It was something about the flapping of their wings that always got me. I mean, it was beautiful to know they were there, but you couldn't really see them when they were airborne. You just had to trust that they were there.

"Maribella, did you remember to bring my sewing kit?" I had asked her to bring it, in case I needed to make some adjustments on Chompers's scarves and blankets.

"Yup, it's in your backpack."

"Maribella, what do you think about Queen Penelope's announcement at the town hall meeting that whoever finds the king will be the next heir to the throne?" Maribella didn't seem to find it interesting at all, from what I caught glimpses of at the meeting. How could she not be? It was a chance to be on the inside and bring forth change. Plus, I would have all the finest clothes at my disposal and a team around me to make sure I always looked my best. It felt almost like the opportunity for a fairy tale was at the feet of anyone who ever dreamt of living in the lap of luxury.

"Eh."

Eh? That's all I get? Did Maribella have no interest in having her life change in an instant?

"I mean, it would be great and all, but what am I going to do? I have no fighting skills, and I am too afraid to really put myself out there to fight. I think I might just run, even if I felt danger nearby. Also, do you think that King Tia might be doing some kind of publicity stunt?"

"What do you mean?"

"I mean, why all of a sudden has he gone missing? It doesn't make sense."

Maribella had me thinking about what King Tia might really be up to—and the whole castle for that matter. That was the good thing about Maribella. She had these moments of genius that only came from going against the grain.

"Plus, think about it. This might just be their way of creating some flamboyant story. Who knows if they are really going to stick to their words. Even if they do, Johnny Jester or someone like him will more than likely be taking over the throne. They need strong men and women. Not us."

We're strong, I thought. Maribella's words dug into me. How could she think that I wasn't strong? Perhaps not physically, but I had my strengths. Didn't I?

We hopped over the fence and headed toward the willow tree. It got quiet between Maribella and me as her words began to sink in. My dad's words started to linger in my mind about staying on path. What did Dad mean by that?

"Chompers!" I shouted as we settled near the burnaberry tree where he usually met us.

"Chompers!" Maribella and I both shouted into the cold air. There was nothing living in sight near us. The snow covered the forest ground, leaving just the trees to stand tall.

"Alistar, should we go back? I don't see Chompers here, and it's getting cold." The temperature had really dropped. We were doing this for Chompers. He knew us and needed our help, even if he didn't know it at the time. Plus, dragging all these blankets back home in defeat didn't feel like an option.

"One moment," I said to Maribella. I placed my backpack on the ground and dug out the breakfast burrito.

"Chompers!" I called once more. *He's alive, I know he's alive.* I hoped the smell of breakfast burritos would catch his attention.

"Did you see that?"

I looked around, seeing no one.

"Someone is here." Maribella, now leaning into me, grabbed my hand as we stood in the white forest with the blankets overflowing out of my backpack.

"There it is again," Maribella remarked.

I could see what Maribella was talking about now. A dark figure was edging toward us from the distance. *Could that be King Tia? He has a crown on and his velvet cloak.* From a distance, it looked like he walked on all fours. Maribella looked at me in fear. There was no running, hiding, or climbing. What had I gotten us into? *I should have stayed on the path just like Dad always said.* Every part of my body was stricken with fear, and I knew that the end was near. This was why they said not to go into Hummingbird Forest.

CHAPTER 13
Conflict

Feud Rise

"She's gone,"
They whimpered
With sorrow so deep.
"We're lost without her.
We need you to keep."
He looked at his tribe
And said, "Worry no more.
I will be your father.
He soon shall implore."

I t was freezing, and the snow was beginning to pick up as we looked into the creature's dark, beady eyes. I could feel Maribella's warm paw squeeze mine.

"Do you know where you are, boy?" he asked. The grizzly bear appeared to be about four feet tall and seven hundred pounds.

"Yes," I said as my heart raced. He looked a bit disheveled to me as he wore King Tia's crown. King Tia was much, much smaller than him, so I couldn't imagine how tight his garments must have felt on him. I had never seen a grizzly bear that close before. Dad always said to play dead if one came near, but it was too late for that since he had spotted us from a distance.

"My friends tell me that they see you here in my forest often. Can you tell me what you do here, boy?"

Although stricken with fear, I found it odd that he kept calling me *boy*. It reminded me of something my P.E. teacher, Mr. Kranagan, would do. He was always referring to us as boys and girls and never by our names. It always irked me.

"My name is Alistar, and this is Maribella. I usually come here to get burnaberries to feed my raganoo, Chompers." I could feel the tension rise among us. I dared to speak my name when I wasn't asked in a time that required me to follow orders intently.

"Ah … Alistar. What an interesting name. My name is Barnty. I am known around here as the keeper of bees, and you are here, trespassing on my land." I didn't know that part of Hummingbird Forest was secluded. So I didn't know if what Barnty was telling me was true. I just listened to him speak because that was all I could do.

"Boys and girls, what do we do to creatures who trespass?" Maribella and I heard it, and there was no mistake. They had risen from the grasps of King Tia. A swarm of honeybees had come to Barnty's side and began buzzing around his ears.

"Ah, yes, yes, yes," said Barnty in excitement. "Yes. I hear you, my children. You are all so right, but let us not harm them just yet.

"Well, Alistar and Maribella. It looks like you'll be coming with us."

"Get in motion," Barnty said to the bees. They began to swarm around Maribella and me and settled right behind us, pointing their stingers at our backs. There were probably thousands of them all aligned perfectly behind us. If we move one inch backward, we would be stung with a thousand stings, which would instantly paralyze both Maribella and me.

"One wrong move, and all will go down the tubes," Barnty warned Maribella and me. We were both freezing cold as Barnty and his army of bees led us deeper and deeper into Hummingbird Forest. I held Maribella's hand to comfort her as we walked to our unknown destination.

"It's going to be all right," I whispered to Maribella, although I didn't know it. Her hand kept shaking, and her head hung down as we walked along, led by Barnty.

We approached a small, dark cave, and the buzzing grew louder.

"Children, children, you will quiet down now," Barnty commanded his swarm of bees. They just grew louder and louder. Barnty began to become agitated, swatting his paws around, trying to gain control of the bees.

"I command all of you to be quiet *now*!" he shouted into the misty air. The bees, although they led us through the cold winter day to the cave, didn't seem to want to take orders from Barnty now.

The buzzing grew louder and louder as the bees broke formation and now swarmed around Barnty. "Out of here, all of you! I've had enough! I didn't ask to be here." The bees began to calm down and headed back into the forest.

What did Barnty mean when he said that he didn't ask to be here? Again, I began to look at Barnty. He looked tired, like he needed a good nap. He probably wasn't used to staying awake during the winter. We had learned in Mr. Wendon's class that bears usually sleep during the cold months.

"I don't want to do this to you, guys, but I have no choice. Come with me."

Barnty led us deep into the hollow cave. There were pots and pots of honey along the walls. He lived in a shabby old place with just the bare minimum of things. Maribella and I stayed quiet, just looking around and listening to Barnty as he spoke from time to time.

"You know, Alistar and Maribella, I didn't want to do this." Maribella and I both looked at each other, exchanging confused glances.

"I get it. I know you're not here to harm anyone, but I must do what they say. I will not kill, although they would like me to. That's where I draw the line."

Was he talking about the bees? Why were they controlling him? Didn't he claim to be the keeper of bees, whatever that meant?

"You see, Alistar and Maribella, I had to step into this role to watch out for the honeybees. They supply me with so much honey to help me get through my days of hibernation. One day I'm sitting in Hummingbird Forest, eating the plethora of honey they have provided me, when I hear the swarming screams of the honeybees approaching. There are thousands and thousands of them gathering around the sunflower field, and as I approached closer, I saw it." Barnty had led us into the deep caverns of his home. It was dark in there, and Maribella and I could only see his eyes as he spoke.

"The queen lay on top of the sunflower with her wings clipped and her spirit gone. The cries of the honeybees is one I'll never forget. They came to me that day, telling me about King Tia's honey farm and all of his acts of merciless killings. They've watched from high and low the greed that led to treating my children as products, and I cannot stand by that. So they claimed me as their father, for they see me as big and strong. We plan to capture the king and anyone who does us harm. In the night, they quietly filed into King Tia's bedroom and lifted him slowly as he soundly slept on his sheets. In the whisper of the night, they brought him to me."

I had known of King Tia's honey farm but never understood how deeply he cut into the lives of every honeybee. They were afraid of him.

"The bees are mad. I can't hide that, and they are scared. They demand capture of every creature if they feel even a hint of danger. They want them caught and brought to justice. They don't want another one of their lives gone because of the carelessness of someone bigger and stronger than they are. So that is why I've brought you here. I must make them feel safe, for they provide the world with what we need, and it is not right of King Tia to use them for his own greed."

Barnty stood in silence for one moment. He directed Maribella and me to step into what seemed to be a jailhouse made of solid wood. He locked the doors and lit a candle before stepping out of the room. Maribella and I looked around the dimly lit cage and screamed in terror.

"Alistar, he's dead," Maribella whimpered.

CHAPTER 14

A Glimpse of Light

H e looked so different to us. Stripped down to his white T-shirt and boxers, I didn't recognize the great King Tia that had walked into Mr. Wendon's class a few months ago. I could see he was badly hurt. His gray fur was covered with dirt and matted. The king seemed to have been stung and lay nearly lifeless on the ground.

"He's breathing," Maribella said. We saw his chest rise and fall, giving us a sense of hope.

"Is there water?" I looked around the small cage for something to revive King Tia. Barnty had left King Tia a small bowl of honey and a small bowl of water. I grabbed the bowl of water and brought it closer to King Tia.

"King Tia, are you okay?" I placed one paw on his shoulder. I could tell he was in pain as he squinted his eyes, trying to focus his gaze on Maribella and me.

"Alistar? Alistar Sparks? Is that you?" King Tia was beginning to wake up and sat upright.

"Yes, it's me, King Tia. I am here with Maribella. Are you okay?"

It felt like such an odd thing to ask. I knew nothing about this way okay. King Tia had been kidnapped from his castle and brought to the deepest parts of Hummingbird Forest to be held as a prisoner, and he looked far from okay.

"I'm afraid, Alistar. I fear for my life. I fear for my family, and I fear for the future of the kingdom." It was so strange to hear King Tia say that he feared for the kingdom when so many feared him.

"I want to tell you things will get better, and I want to give you some hope, but I cannot do that. These bees are angry—and furiously so." I could see the pain in King Tia's eyes as they filled with tears as he spoke.

"They are out of control. Their leader, Barnty, thinks he has control over them, but he doesn't. They don't listen to him. He thinks they do. I hear him frustrated day in and day out. He throws the pots of honey around the cave in frustration after they leave. I know I killed their queen, and that's why I'm here today. I wish I could take back what I've done, but I can't." Tears rolled down King Tia's face. I truly believed that he did understand what his actions had caused, but did he deserve a life of being locked away from his family? I couldn't imagine King Tia never seeing his wife again. Although I did not care for King Tia's actions toward me on presentation day, I knew he was deeply sorrowful for what happened, and I believed he could change. I began to wonder if we could ever leave. I believed there was a way. Then, like a perfect snowstorm, the idea of a way out began to form in my mind.

CHAPTER 15
Puppet Villain

The next couple of days were rough. As the bees would come in and out of the cave, they would taunt Maribella, King Tia, and me. We were afraid we would be stung by a thousand bees and would not be able to survive. It was interesting that something so small could cause so much pain, and they were traveling in groups.

Barnty would come and check on us from time to time. I could tell he cared but didn't want to disobey the bees, although he called himself the keeper of bees.

"How's the honey?" Barnty asked one day as he sat in the back of the cave with us. King Tia's crown looked worn down, and Barnty looked extremely uncomfortable in his attire.

"The honey is good," Maribella and I answered. King Tia spent most of his time sleeping. The bees were angered by him the most and came to taunt him as they pleased. He found that if he pretended to be asleep and not make a sound, they would leave him alone for a short while.

I couldn't help but think back to what Barnty said—that he didn't ask for this.

"Barnty, can I ask you something?" Barnty looked in my direction, silently giving me permission through his eyes to speak.

"What did you mean when you said that you didn't ask for this?"

The question intrigued him. He got up from his chair and stepped closer to the jailhouse that we all sat in.

"I didn't ask for this. Yes, this is true," Barnty said in sorrow. "I try to do everything for my children, and they come back and want more. I try to look the part and act the part. I thought by dressing in a crown and King Tia's velvet cloak, they would see me as an authority figure, that the children that asked me to be here would finally take me seriously. They asked me to be here. I am here today trying to carry them forward, but I feel like I'm grasping at straws."

"Why don't you just leave?" I asked, testing the waters with Barnty.

"Is that what you want?" Barnty asked, looking deep into my eyes. I could tell that part of Barnty wanted to let us go but also that he wouldn't go against his tribe.

"Yes. If you let us go, you'll have a place to stay in Carrot Kingdom," I persisted. I just needed to know where we stood with Barnty. The bees were gone for most of the day, so he did have the power if he chose.

"I simply don't see that ever happening," Barnty said, smiling. It was like he too, on some level, enjoyed seeing us trapped in a cage. This was a side to him I hadn't seen. "What King Tia did was inexcusable. There were so many lives lost in his years of owning his honey farm, and like trash, the bees were thrown away. They are angered by this. They feel he is a threat, and they don't ever want to see him go. I am their savior and will stand by their side."

I looked over at Maribella, and as Barnty spoke, I could see that the glimpse of hope she once held in her eyes had dissipated. She sat down in a corner and stared into her paws, as if trying to see what the future might be. It was odd to see Maribella and King Tia in this state. When

Barnty spoke, I felt as though there was still hope, but I didn't feel like he was going to let us go prancing out the door. *What could we do?* As I sat on the damp cave floor and rested my head against the wall, an idea began to unravel in my mind of the perfect way to escape Barnty and his army of bees.

I opened up my backpack and pulled out my sketchbook, colored pencils, my mother's knitting kit, and every art supply I had sitting in my bag. It was time to get to work.

CHAPTER 16
The Magic Sparks

It had been seven days since I had seen my dad. I kept thinking about what he must be going through, what Maribella's mom and Queen Penelope were going through. I imagined him coming home from work during his lunch break to find Maribella and I were not there. He would have to tell Maribella's mother and alert the castle. It was everything my dad never asked for, and I had put him there. It was interesting how much sorrow selfishness brought. One decision I had made for Maribella and me had led us there into the cave.

"What are you doing, Alistar?" Maribella asked as she woke up. King Tia was still asleep. I thought it best not to wake him. Sleep was where he found his sense of peace for now. Maribella and I could hear him cry himself to sleep the past couple of days. He needed this time to rejuvenate.

I had dug into my mom's knitting kit. The acrylic box she gave me on my birthday had all kinds of yarn in it. I spent the night knitting away.

"That's never going to work, Alistar," Maribella said, sliding right next to me as I put the finishing touches on the outfits.

"Maribella, you forget. It's all about the details," I said, smiling. I could not tell the future, and I did not know if it was going to work. I hoped it would. I felt like we had run out of options, and this was what I thought could work in the best way possible.

I remembered the taunts of Johnny Jester as I worked on the four greatest creations of my life. Maribella and I had been walking to school, and I specifically remembered her telling me that Johnny didn't understand, that he was not like us.

Although I knew it was a long shot, I was willing to try anything at this stage. It was about five thirty in the morning, and we heard the bees head out of the cave. It was during this time that Barnty was getting ready to come check on us. Like clockwork, he always came to see us right after the honeybees left to work for the day.

"King Tia, wake up," I said. "Wear this." I threw him an outfit. I put mine on and placed Maribella's on her as well.

We saw his dark shadow enter the back of the cave. The candle had burned out in the night, but there was a small hole at the top of the cave that allowed some light to enter in.

Barnty stood by a small, round table and lit the candle to bring some light into our dark room.

"What are you wearing?" Barnty asked, intrigued, now walking closer to our cage.

Through the night, I had knitted four outfits, all to resemble what a honeybee's coat would look like. I had a ton of yellow and black yarn for our body suits and a little black cap for each of us to wear.

All three of us stood in a bee line. It was important for us to sink into the culture of bee life at this moment.

"I was thinking about what you said and about all the horrible things King Tia has done to the honeybees. He understands now how important it is to not hurt another being. I've talked to King Tia, and we are going to be by your side." I was telling a small white lie, but Barnty had left us no choice. Maribella and I hadn't asked to be there, nor had we done any harm, but there we were—trapped in the horrible mess of brewing feuds.

"I made one for you too," I said to Barnty. I could see a glimmer of excitement in his eyes. He tried to hold it back but failed miserably to do so. I could tell a lot by the way he looked at the outfit. It was everything he was looking for. King Tia's outfit was poorly constructed on him, and he didn't quite fit in with the bees, as he mentioned. No, he needed this outfit. He needed to be one of them and to show it externally, and this beautiful piece was going to do that for him.

"I still have some measuring to do, but I was able to eyeball it. If you let me out of the cage, I can measure you properly and add the jewels. I know that you said you felt like the bees weren't listening to you, and I think it's because you don't look like them. If you wear this outfit as a peace offering from us, I think it could enforce your authority as the leader and their beekeeper."

Barnty stared at all three of us, pondering the idea of letting us out for a moment. He could easily catch us. We were three small rabbits compared to him, so it wouldn't be hard. I could feel my heart begin to race at the idea of freedom coming closer. *Three deep breaths,* I thought. It was the quickest way to get me back to being grounded and on track. Maribella and King Tia were now counting on me.

"Okay, just you," Barnty said. "The other two need to stay in the cage."

I brought out the bright yellow and black striped outfit for him. It was cylindrical in shape. I used black glitter for the black stripes to give it an extra pop. I wanted Barnty to blend in but also stand out. He looked at the outfit with so much joy in his eyes.

"Let me put it on you. You'll have to kneel down." I stood up on a tall chair that Barnty had in the back of the cave and slipped on the outfit from the top. It looked like a tube made of the finest yarn. Mom always bought the highest-quality supplies from Mr. Toddly's House of Arts and Crafts. Dad said she believed in the durability of the product. It was an interesting process to knit the outfits through the night. I worked fast, and Barnty's took the longest. You start with two needles and piece of yarn. Now to look at a single string of yarn, it looks fragile and weak. However, as you put it into motion and start looping the yarn with the help of the needles, it becomes fabric. A durable piece of fabric that you can use to create anything you desire. Now, this wouldn't have been possible without the string of yarn, and alone, it wouldn't be able to do what I wished to accomplish next.

Barnty was strong. I could feel it as I jumped down from the chair and pulled the remaining part of the outfit to his knees.

"I'm going to cut the part for the arms in just a second." I had purposely left out a place for Barnty to pull his arms through.

Barnty stood up and looked at himself in the mirror. He was so happy to see himself shining in the bright yellow outfit. He looked just like his colony of bees. Now he could truly say to them he was the keeper of the bees.

I looked back at Maribella and nodded.

"Okay, Barnty. Now time for the arms," I said and asked him to sit on the chair. He looked like a butterfly stuck in a cocoon of brightly colored yellow and black fabric. I felt bad for Barnty because this isn't what I wanted. I wished there was another way, but he had no intention of letting us go.

"I'm sorry, Barnty," I said. Barnty looked confused, completely unaware as he tried to stand up but could not. His arms were stuck inside the outfit that I promised I would cut. He struggled and struggled but could not break through the tightly knitted fabric. The outfit left him paralyzed.

"Come on, Maribella and King Tia! We need to go now!" I unlocked the cage and led them through the darkness of the cave. It was light out, and I could see the morning sun rising. The bees were nowhere in sight, but I could hear them buzzing nearby. We ran for a while back toward the willow tree.

"Chompers!" I shouted. I figured the bees must have heard us because the buzzing became louder and louder. "Chompers! Chompers! Chompers!" The buzzing grew louder, and I could tell they were nearing. Maribella held my hand, and King Tia looked around the sky as we began to see a swarm of bees nearing by.

Chompers appeared out the bushes near the willow tree, and we all hopped on his back.

"Hold tight!" I said to the king and Maribella.

"Chompers, are you ready? Let's go!" I clicked my feet against his feathery side, and we began to lift up into the air. Maribella held onto my waist, and King Tia kept his eyes closed as we soared higher and higher into the sky.

"King Tia, you can open your eyes now. We are okay." The king slowly opened his eyes to see that we were all right, flying away from the cave and toward the kingdom.

"Alistar! They are right behind us!" Maribella squealed.

The bees must have become aware that we were on the verge of escaping. I could see a small swarm of bees tailing behind us.

Bzzzzzzzzz bzzzzzzz bzzzzzzz.

"Ouch!" Maribella began to scream. King Tia closed his eyes once more and leaned into Chompers, trying to get away from the bees now swarming and attacking Maribella and King Tia.

"Chompers, faster!" I said, and like the speed of light, we began to lose the swarm of bees. They became tiny little dots and soon disappeared into the forest.

"Phew, that was close!" I said to Maribella and King Tia. My heart was racing. *Three deep breaths.* We were nowhere near Hummingbird Forest any longer and now could see the lay of the land beneath us of Carrot Kingdom. The creatures looked so small from up there. We were now safe and headed back to the palace.

CHAPTER 17

A Vision Blooms

I t was such an odd feeling, not waking up in my room. The sheets were heavy and luxurious, made of the finest silks and golden embroidery that told a very special story of Carrot Kingdom. The walls were painted a mellow yellow with hints of gold crown molding. The floors were made of black and white tiles. Everything in the room jumped out at me with its vintage and artistic flare. I looked out the window at the kingdom and thought of all the colorful changes I wanted to bring.

"Alistar, are you up?" my dad said, walking into my new room. We were now living at the castle where King Tia and Queen Penelope resided. King Tia had stepped down from the throne, as Queen Penelope said he would.

"Yeah, Dad. I'm awake."

"Are you ready for today?" he asked, gleaming with so much pride.

It was so nice to see my dad happy. I don't think he ever imagined we would end up ruling the kingdom. The morning we escaped from the grasps of Barnty and the bees, I had Chompers take us to the castle.

There was a huge thud as he landed on the balcony. Dad and Queen Penelope were having tea, and it looked like they were discussing a plan for more search parties.

They both came out to find all three of us on a raganoo. Dad hugged me right away, and the queen summoned for Maribella's mother to come to the castle. They were all happy that we were okay. King Tia, though, couldn't find happiness right away. He hugged Queen Penelope, went into his room, and closed the door for a few days. We could hear him crying in the night. I think he finally realized what he had done, and the overwhelming guilt seemed to consume him. Although it was a happy time, sorrow still followed.

We went on to tell the queen and Dad about Barnty and the bees and the discovery of what may have happened to the other royals. They both listened intently.

Today was going to be interesting because I was being inducted into the castle as the new king, and Maribella would be on the creative committee. She first resisted and said no when I asked, but the intrigue was too much when she thought about where creativity could lead us.

"I'll just need a few moments, Dad, and I'll be right out." I got out of bed and hopped in the shower. There was a designer there by the name of Corina. She laid out a brightly colored purple velvet suit with pink, purple, yellow, and blue jewels.

I stepped onto the balcony and looked out into the masses. It was a bright, sunny day, and the skies were clear. Everyone had traveled from near and far for this day. It was one to go down in the history books. A boy saved the king using his creative side. There were always tons of war stories being told that included duels between two sides using swords and battle gear. There were always casualties. Whoever sat on the throne showed consistent marks on the battlefield, successfully bringing the enemies down, but here I stood in front of a crown, having taken a very different route. King Tia began to speak.

"Today it is my honor and pleasure to bring you the new king of

Carrot Kingdom. His name is Alistar Sparks. Alistar showed great courage, creativity, and quick thinking in my time of need. I had been gone for weeks, with no hope in sight. Captured by the very creatures that I imprisoned and tormented. I had made peace with the possibility that I would never return to the kingdom. You see, I was taken hostage by the keeper of bees, Barnty, for my wrongdoings to his children, and although I see that the punishment did fit the crime, I did not want my life to end. When I saw them bring in Alistar, I thought all three of us were going to die. He came in with the courage and perseverance needed to get us out, and he believed he could do this. Alistar used his creativity to get us home, and it's what our kingdom needs. So, with no further delay, here is your new king."

I stepped farther out onto the balcony and looked at the crowd. They were all cheering for me. I thought of how Mom would be so proud. Dad was shooting away on his camera, taking pictures of every moment. I didn't know exactly how to be a king or what steps to take next. None of that mattered to me in that moment. I knew where we were heading, and the first step was to reform the bonds of the broken ties left by the other kingdoms. It was time to bring King Zazar's dream of colorful beauty back to life. It was time we listened to what the people wanted. My heart filled with joy, knowing that things were about to change not just for Creatopia but for every little boy and girl who desired to follow their passion.

A Key Player

Through the gated shrubs of Palace Pond, King Hently leapt out into Hummingbird Forest and left his kingdom behind. Rushing through the forest, frantically looking from left to right, he could feel his heart nearly beating out of his chest.

Hop, hop, hop.

Now where is it? I don't see it, King Hently thought. There was no stopping now. He had fear in his heart of what was to come if he didn't succeed.

Could that be it? King Hently wondered as he approached a giant willow tree. He knew that this was the tree he had been searching for as he made his way toward the enormous willow. As he looked up at the tree, he could not tell where it ended and where the sky began. The branches drooped down to the ground, carrying the teardrop leaves along. He could not help but think of the sorrow that filled the atmosphere around such a prominent figure. It did not seem to match the land it sat on, as he was in Hummingbird Forest, filled with enchantingly bright flowers and tropical, exotic fruits. The Ministry had been working hard to keep the forest filled with colorful beauty, but here stood one of the oldest trees in Creatopia with haunting sadness.

King Hently's journey began with a mysterious vial left on his windowsill in the middle of the night. He was abruptly woken from a dream when he heard a small *clink* as something dropped near his window. He rushed to see what was left when he caught the sight of a mysterious dark figure disappearing into the night on a raganoo. He picked up the peculiar vial filled with pink, bubbling fluid. Attached to the vial was a note that said "drink me" with the sign of the lemur embossed on the cap.

No ... this can't be. He's gone. This vial came directly from the Ministry of Creatopia and belonged to King Zazar. Curious about what was to come from the drink, King Hently opened the cap on the vial and began to drink the pink, bubbly fluid. Like a black-and-white movie, a vision of his father flashed before his eyes.

"It's like a dance between you and the fly. There is tension in the air, but if you really want it, you can quiet your mind and focus, my son. Patience is the way," his father urged. They were in their backyard getting ready for supper when his father decided it was time to teach his son how to catch a fly. If he could catch a fly, he could do *anything*.

"See that one there?"

He pointed to a fly that was nearing closer to them. "What you want to do is focus. He is going to move, but if you stay still enough, you will clear the air of worry. Stay still ... and now!" The father's tongue leapt out of his mouth and into the air, catching the fly.

"See! Okay. Your turn."

Hently now turned his focus to the next fly that seemed to enter their parameter.

"Okay, son ... focus. Be still, and just when you feel a calmness through your body, I want you to do exactly as I did."

Hently focused in. The fly began to move away slowly. *Oh, no, it's getting away,* he thought. He then tried to catch the fly with his tongue quickly. The fly disappeared into the distance.

"Son, you've got to wait. Patience is key."

"Come on, you two." Hently's mother began calling them both inside, back into the palace.

The memories of his father and mother filtered away as the cold breeze flushed across his face and he was brought back into his reality. He looked up at the gigantic willow tree.

"Hello! Anybody there? You called me to come, so I'm here," he said into the night air, hoping someone could hear him.

"Hello? Again, Weeping Willow, I'm here. What is it that you want?" King Hently said to the willow tree and received absolute silence. The night sky seemed darker than usual as Hently looked up at the stars for relief and light. None were to be seen. It was as if the stars of the universe had disappeared and were going to leave him and the tree in the dark of the night.

He took a deep breath and was filled with annoyance when he felt the ground begin to break. The roots of the willow tree had awakened and broke through the ground now, wrapping around King Hently and lifting him off the ground.

A face appeared in the bark of the willow tree as it brought King Hently closer to it.

"Ahhh … you …"

The willow tree had emerald-green eyes, and its lips were made of bark.

"You …" the willow tree whispered as it looked deep into King Hently's eyes.

King Hently gulped in horror. He could feel the branches tightening their grip around his waist.

"Yes, it's me." King Hently managed to spit out his words. "Why am I here?"

"You …" the willow tree whispered again.

King Hently felt helpless, looking out into the night sky. He was trapped in the grips of the willow tree. *Is this the end? Am I going to die here in the night with no one around me?* Frantically looking around, he saw a peculiar object flying near him at an alarming speed. As it got closer, a shape began to appear. A hummingbird, it appeared to be. Hently had never seen one so closely before. Its wings nearly disappeared into the air as it flapped about near him. The hummingbird was from the Ministry of Creatopia. He was dressed in a tiny, maroon, velvet vest that hugged his small, blue, smooth feathers. On the vest, there was gold embroidery with three colorful jewels in the shape of a white rose. The white rose symbolized purity and love. According to the Ministry, that was the symbol they chose to honor King Zazar's departure from Creatopia.

"Hi. I'm from the Ministry of Creatopia, and I believe you're Hently, the king of Palace Pond? You can call me Yogi. My friends just refer to me as Yog. I got a little bit of training to do before I let you into the Forbidden Forest." When Yogi spoke, he seemed nervous, avoiding eye contact and periodically looking to the ground.

"You're King Hently, right? Oh yeah, I've heard so much about you! Did you imprison the blue-eyed rabbit who was stealing all the fresh water lilies?"

King Hently chuckled as he responded, "Yes, that was me! The little bugger tried to take every beautiful lily we had in sight." He was beginning to feel more at ease.

"Hey, big boy. You can let him go now," Yogi instructed. The willow tree dropped Hently to the ground. He was feeling relieved now that Yogi was there.

"Oh … a … what happened to him? We heard you didn't let him go," Yogi said.

"Well, yeah," Hently said with a glimmer of pride in his eyes. "You come to my palace, take my lilies, and don't think you're going to get away with it. You surely have another thing coming."

"I heard through the grapevine that he was trying to create some artwork to support his family."

"Artwork? Since when has that ever been important? How I see it is that the blue-eyed rabbit stole from me and my dream of seeing a plethora of lilies, and that's plain wrong."

"Hmm." Yogi had a questioning look in his eyes as King Hently's words melted into him.

"Yes," Yogi said, "that is *true*. We can begin the training now."

Hently felt the mood had suddenly shifted between Yogi and him, as if he had played into some part of his plot.

"Let us get started now," Yogi said with power and direction in his voice. "First off, do you know why you're here?"

"Yeah, I was left a note to come to the willow tree. It had late King Zazar's symbol on it of the half moon. It was inside a vial of bubbling pink fluid that I was instructed to drink."

"Yes. Along with you, there have been others who were sent vials of various bubbling fluids. They should be arriving soon. The spirit of King Zazar has awoken, and he is calling out to all to restore the vision of Creatopia. You have been assigned King Tia, who has gone missing. You are to help a little boy named Alistar bring him back to the kingdom. Once you complete this mission, you will journey to Narwhal Landing. There you will find another like Alistar that needs your help."

To be continued …

About the Author

Reema, a first-generation American whose family immigrated from the Fijian islands, grew up in a small town within the California Bay Area. She obtained her bachelor's degree in criminal justice and has spent a number of years as a life coach. When she's not writing, she enjoys sketching, cooking, and spending time with family and friends.

CPSIA information can be obtained
at www.ICGtesting.com
Printed in the USA
BVHW032112250320
576011BV00007B/27/J